TREACHERY AT ROCK POINT

Peter Dawson

G.K. Hall & Co. • Thorndike, Maine

Published in 1999 by arrangement with Golden West Literary Agency.

G.K. Hall Large Print Paperback Series.

The text of this Large Print edition is unabridged.
Other aspects of the book may vary from the original edition.

Set in 16 pt. Plantin by Al Chase.

Printed in the United States on permanent paper.

Library of Congress Cataloging in Publication Data

Dawson, Peter, 1907–
    Treachery at Rock Point / Peter Dawson.
      p.   cm.
    ISBN 0-7838-8493-1 (lg. print : sc : alk. paper)
    1. Large type books. I. Title.
    [PS3507.A848T74 1999]
    813'.54—dc21
                                          98-48261

TREACHERY
AT ROCK POINT

ONE

The roustabouts were ashore at the first hint of false dawn, casting loose the lines that had held the *Belle* moored against the pull of the Missouri's sluggish current throughout the night. And shortly the ring of a bell below, the swish of the big paddle wheel astern and the gentle chuffing of the boilers roused a tall, lean-hipped man who had slept out the night close to the rail on the riverward side of the main deck.

He tossed his blankets aside, came lazily erect and stretched his buckskin-clad frame. Yawning prodigiously, he ran a hand over his short chestnut-red beard, afterward stepping over to climb the ladder to the hurricane, moving lithely and with complete ease. Above, he sauntered across the unlighted deck to stand alongside the wheelhouse platform and scan the surrounding darkness, feeling the bite in the chill air of this mid-September morning.

To watch and listen to the coming of each new day invariably brought its strong pleasure to this erect, wide-shouldered man. Yet this particular morning his relishing of what the thinning blackness gradually disclosed was doubly satisfying. For it lacked but one month of being two years since he had last set eyes upon this night-shrouded sweep of range he called home.

So strong was his eagerness to glimpse it that, for the first time in the five days since he had come aboard the *Belle*, he could push to the back of his mind a myriad of frustrating and unwanted memories — the lingering feel of utter exhaustion, the nightmare images of scalped and mutilated bodies, the haunting drumfire crackle of hot carbines fired in anger and desperation.

This was Will Speer, five weeks out of a Fort Lapwai infirmary bed, his left shoulder still faintly tender from the punishment given it by a Nez Perce bullet.

Disgust had been strong in him that day when, on drawing his final pay as a civilian scout for General Howard, he had bought a horse, left the reservation behind him and headed down the Clearwater along the line of the distant Bitter Root peaks.

His disgust had been bred by the ineptness of command that had caused the loss of an entire troop of the First Cavalry to the ambushing guns of Joseph, the wily Nez Perce chief. That troop had comprised half the force he had been serving with back in June when the bullet brought him down — along with dozens of blue-clad troopers — in the depths of White Bird Canyon, hard above the Salmon River.

By now that disgust had become resignation. It had worn itself out to the point where he could summon scarcely a trace of the rancor that had been in him three months ago. All that lay behind him; he had closed the book on it. He

8

was back home; and this was the morning he had been yearning for over these many interminable weeks.

He stepped onto the platform now and across to the open window of the wheelhouse, the deep gloom barely letting him make out the shape of the man at the head-high wheel. The packet was little more than drifting with the current, her stern wheel churning slowly, barely giving her steerageway.

Will Speer, not understanding this as he thought back and remembered where they had tied up for the night, remarked, "You've got three, four miles of deep water ahead, Hargutt."

The wheelman hawked, clearing his throat before dryly stating, "And snags, too. Damn freshet up Mule Ear washed out a jag o' timber back in April. So we wait'll the light's better before we try and make time."

"What'll it be, eight o'clock before we make the Point?"

"Be a safer bet to call it nine."

Will Speer turned away, hunkering down with his back to the wheelhouse's front corner and taking out pipe and tobacco. The pipe alight, he stared ahead between the two pairs of towering spars beyond the forward edge of the deck, watching the strengthening light heighten the paleness of the river's gray surface.

Presently, the sudden screeching of a jay from a willow brake along the near bank shattered the stillness and caught his attention. His glance had barely swung in that direction before he was seeing the shadowy forms of a band of antelope bounding away into the obscurity. *Loafer wolf*, he thought idly as he once again eyed the broad ribbon of the river up ahead.

In forty more minutes he was hungrily watching the sun's brassy disk edge over the far, familiar horizon. And as that first blaze of light touched the land he took in the beauty of the cloudless morning with a feeling of wonder and awe at his ever having turned his back upon this country.

The hazed and jagged ramparts of the Arrowheads lay in the northward distance, their higher crests already wearing pale caps of white to signal the approach of winter. To the east, ahead, low rims flanked the river basin, while off to the south rolled timbered hills pocketed with open parks.

That vast sweep of rising grassland just below the southeastern horizon would be Crow Track's home meadow.

He was acutely aware of his glance having been irresistibly drawn to the meadow, and sight of it brought him a restless feeling of unease. He had been unconsciously bracing himself for this moment, yet anxious to face it. And now as the uneasiness slowly died away, leaving him unruffled and no more than mildly interested in what he was seeing, he dryly told himself, *You've grown up, man. Wouldn't even matter if they're married.*

Some subtle transformation had taken place deep within him over these past few seconds. And it was with a keen relief that he realized his long absence had worked the much-needed alchemy of leaving him with a changed outlook. In his mind's eye he could summon up the vision of a fair and dark-haired young woman and remember her only with tenderness and affection, and not with futile longing.

For the first time he could look back across the past two years and really believe they hadn't been wasted.

He came erect with the satisfying sense of somehow having been cleansed of an unwanted and time-hardened bitterness. Such an emotion had always been foreign to his nature; to know that he was finally rid of it was like rising from a sickbed after a long fever.

From below now he occasionally caught the sound of voices, and shortly he was hearing the gruff cursing of the mate sounding up from the main deck as the man ordered the roustabouts to the shifting of freight to be unloaded at Rock Point. The *Belle* was coming awake.

In several more minutes the light breeze wafted to him the tantalizing aroma of coffee and frying bacon. All at once ravenous, Will Speer swung down the ladder to the deck below.

The three-tiered streets of Rock Point were alive with a heavy traffic even at this early hour, just short of nine o'clock. Four team ore wagons, headed for the mill out at the end of Front Street down along the river, rolled along paying scant respect to the right of way of lesser rigs — buckboards, flatbed wagons, a scattering of surreys and buggies.

Caroline Knight reined her bay horse aside and hard against her father's sorrel in getting out of the way of the lead team of one of the Oriole mine's high-bodied wagons overtaking them, thus avoiding being run down.

Her parent, eyes blazing, stood in the stirrups and bawled a ripe oath, shouting to the driver, "Harness 'em side by side and you could take over the walks!"

The girl quickly reached across to lay a restraining hand on his arm. "Easy, Tom. He's half your age and almost as big. You've got to learn to get along with these roughnecks."

"Gold!" Tom Knight blazed. "Why couldn't they have found it at the other end of the Territory?" He gave her a disgusted glance, tilting his head toward a saloon awning and the crowded walk beneath it close ahead. "Things're going to pot. Used to be Charley Forrest didn't have two customers of a morning before eleven. Now look. Bet you he hasn't closed his doors in a month, Sundays included."

"Isn't Charley due his share of this easy money?"

The elder Knight sighed gustily in irritation. "He can have it. Thank the good Lord we don't come in often."

"But I kind of like it." The girl laughed at his scowl of disapproval, afterward shifting her slender figure so as to sit the sidesaddle more comfortably. "Next time we come in though, I'll use my regular rig. This one's hard. And it's too proper."

"Wear pants in front of all this riffraff?"

Caroline assumed a look of mock innocence and reached down to arrange the folds of her russet riding habit. "I'll carry a forty-four if you say, Tom, but pants it is."

"We'll see about that."

Knight's gruff words gave mere lip service to his non-agreement. Well aware of how surely his headstrong daughter took after her mother, who had been in her grave these three years, he accepted the matter as having been settled in Caroline's favor. Father and daughter saw eye to eye on important things, sometimes disagreed on trivialities such as this. So now he consoled himself with the sure understanding that, so long as he held her trust and knew that she had more than her share of plain common sense, he was indeed a fortunate parent.

Presently they were riding down on a gap between one rank of the false-front stores, a long stretch of slab fence bisected by a wide gate with a high archway bearing a new-painted legend:

OAKES and DANBO
BURNT HILLS STAGES
FREIGHT, CONTRACT HAULING

13

And Tom Knight, startled on reading the sign, asked sharply, "So Ned's made Lyle Danbo his partner, Carry?"

The girl, not understanding, followed his glance. Stiffening, she breathed in wonder, "Ned hasn't mentioned it to me."

"He could have waited a decent length of time," Knight caustically remarked.

"For what?"

"Don't know exactly. Only I hate seeing the name changed."

Carry eyed her father obliquely, her look troubled. "So do I. But keeping Will Speer's name on a sign isn't going to bring him back."

Knight shrugged. "You'll be asking Ned to eat dinner with us?"

"Not today. It's Monday. He's riding the Leesville run."

"Forgot." Knight noticed that Carry was still eyeing the wagon yard's sign in strong puzzlement, and the thought struck him, *He doesn't tell her everything, which is damned odd.*

This moment the deep-toned wail of a whistle echoed back from the rocky ridge rising sheerly beyond the eastern edge of town. Cocking his head and listening to the whistle's continuing short blasts, Tom Knight's hawkish face took on a slow, delighted smile. "River boat. Probably the *Belle*. Want to go down and watch her come in?"

"You go, Tom. I have to stop in at the Emporium and pick out that drapery material before

14

they've sold it all."

Knight had an abrupt thought then that made him say, "Y'know, now might be the time to get down to the Elkton ranch with Ned and drive back those mares and geldings. We could ride the *Belle* and be on the river two, three days. You'd come along and share the work."

Carry smiled. "Sounds like a lark. Let's do it."

"Then I'll find out how long the *Belle*'s laying over, if it is the *Belle*."

"Good. See you at the hotel for dinner, will I?" Carry took in her father's nod and added, "Make it by half-past eleven or we get caught in the rush. And I'd thank you not to keep me waiting."

"Never do."

He chuckled at the arch look she gave him and was about to touch the sorrel with spur to pull on ahead when she abruptly said, "And don't worry about the bank, Tom. You and Baker just put your heads together this morning and you'll lick this thing."

"That we will, Carry. Now I'll run along."

He put the sorrel at a brisk jog on down the crowded street, and by the time he had taken the steeply pitched alley from Grant to Front the *Belle* had rounded the upstream bend and was swinging broadside to the current, nosing in toward the levee, making for a point immediately downstream from where the *Star*, Lee Mears's single-stack ferryboat, lay moored in slack water.

Sight of the small but stately stern-wheeler invariably had a strong effect on Tom Knight. He and Ada, Caroline's mother, had four years ago made the trip to Omaha and back on the *Belle*, the purpose of their trip having been to meet Caroline after her graduation in St. Louis from Miss Stanhope's Academy for Gentlewomen.

That had been the late spring and summer before Ada's sudden decline. Memories of the moonlit summer nights and of the many relaxed days with the woman who had meant so much to him, were always strongest when the tidy white-painted packet lay before his eyes, as it did now.

Presently he rode behind a small crowd of townspeople gathered on the levee, then up to the river side of a warehouse, just now preferring his own company to that of others. Coming aground, he watched the *Belle* make the landing close below, the rhythmic pound of the stamp mill downstream laying its discordant mutter as a background to the shouting of the river boat's work gang.

A seedy looking assortment of trappers, Indians, drummers and miners began filing off the wide staging plank once the *Belle* lay moored. Knight eyed the newcomers with strong dislike. He had never ceased regretting the day, fifteen months ago, when Joe Starles had traded his new-found nuggets for a gallon jug of whisky at the War Paint Saloon and thus started the rush up Needle Canyon that climbed through a notch in the ridge three miles to the east of town.

Over that interval of little more than a year,

16

Rock Point had mushroomed from a comfortable and quiet settlement to a bustling, at times bawdy, boom town. As a cattleman and part owner of the town bank, Tom Knight cast a jaundiced eye on all this, seeing the Point's future as being insecure in spite of the bank's increased business, no more stable in fact than the suds on a glass of Charley Forrest's watered-down beer.

Just now a figure moving shoreward along the steamer's stage caught his eye, a figure standing nearly a head taller than the others. He thought, *There comes a big moose,* seeing how easily the big man lugged a saddle, bedroll and scabbarded rifle over one shoulder.

Something about the way the man handled himself, the ease with which he swung aside to let a roustabout past him, gave Knight a twinge. "Looks a little like Will," he mused aloud, adding regretfully, "wish it could be."

He eyed the man more closely, taking in his buckskin shirt and tight pants, his short chestnut-red beard. At length Tom Knight let his breath go in an explosive grunt of strong irritation, forcing himself to look away, to watch the milling figures on the deck moving bales and boxes and barrels toward the shoreward side of the steamer's deck.

But shortly his glance was once more drawn irresistibly back to the tall man, who was now moving through the crowd on the levee. And all at once he dropped the sorrel's reins and hurried

17

out along the embankment, calling stridently, "Will!"

He knew that his voice couldn't be heard over the racket down there. The man in buckskin disappeared behind a dray, and it was when he moved out of sight that Tom Knight slowed his stride, then stopped as he told himself, *Hold on! This one's got a beard. And didn't I read it in the paper with my own eyes? So it can't be.*

In a few more seconds he caught a brief and final glimpse of the man walking toward the long flight of steps that climbed the low bluff to Grant Street. Now he was positive he had been mistaken; and as he turned back to his horse he muttered sheepishly, "Saved yourself from playin' the fool."

Last night's game of high-stake draw poker in the ornate parlor of Lyle Danbo's house on upper Lupin Street had broken up slightly later than usual, not until well after two o'clock. For that reason Danbo was late in shaving and dressing this morning. He was putting the imitation pearl studs in his white pleated shirt when he heard the *Belle* whistle its signal for the landing.

That sound, as always, had a strong and unwelcome effect on Danbo, making him think back across the years to one late spring at Stinkin' Landing, far down the Missouri, when he had been the sole survivor of a group of eight hide-hunters headquartered inside a crude and

18

smelly stockade along the river's bank. The pox had decimated the group, bringing down all but Danbo — who had been stricken with the disease and recovered from it as a youth — and one other, a man well advanced in age.

By the time the runoff had stopped, when a boat made the landing to load upward of four tons of buffalo hides for market, Danbo had simply pointed out the seven wooden crosses in one corner of the small compound. His explanation, never questioned, had taken less than a minute. He had, of course, neglected mentioning that one cross marked the grave of an elderly man who had quite recently died of suffocation following a hard blow on the head.

Those bales of prime hides, sold in Omaha, had marked Lyle Danbo's beginnings as a man of substance. Small in stature and patently unable to make his mark by sheer brawn, the man had used his keen wits along with a remarkably sensitive pair of hands that were equally adept in handling either a gun or a deck of cards. As a gambler, Danbo had long ago learned that skill, not cheating, was the means to a most satisfactory end. He had also learned that a man's winnings varied according to the potential, this being the precise reason he had five months ago picked this boom town as the next in his long series of temporary residences.

Danbo was thirty-four years old. He had been twenty-seven back in '71 when he quit Stinkin' Landing. So unpleasant had been his memories of his life as a hide-hunter — the ever-present stench, the griminess, the flies and the heat, the bitter cold — that he had since come to relish deeply his creature comforts. More than that, he had become truly fastidious in dress and in what he ate, the latter being his reason for permitting himself the luxury of a personal servant, a Negro who cooked for him and looked after his rented house.

This morning as he walked down the hill and turned along Grant Street toward the stage yard, he was nattily outfitted in a black suit and an inconspicuously embroidered gray vest that matched the shade of his derby. His shoes shone with a mirrorlike polish and he wore a fine linen handkerchief in the breast pocket of his coat which bulged slightly from the bulk of a shoulder holster beneath it.

Coming down along the yard's slab fence toward the gate, he glanced up to examine the sign on the high archway which had been painted only yesterday. The lettering was far from perfect, yet he overlooked this in his satisfaction at seeing his name so boldly displayed. He and Ned Oakes had had a slight argument over replacing the name of Speer. Danbo readily understood that Ned attached a certain amount of sentiment to keeping the name. But, as usual in their disagreements, Danbo's cool insistence had finally won out.

He glanced idly back into the big wagon lot as he passed the gate, taking a certain pleasure in thinking of how surely he had deceived Ned in claiming total ignorance of what went on back there. Actually he supposed he knew as much as his new partner did about the workings of the yard. But it didn't interest him particularly. What did interest him, what brought him here on his infrequent visits, was the account books.

Yet just now he couldn't help but notice a thing or two as his glance swung back along the lot. Two men were forking hay from the barn loft into the corral that held upward of a dozen animals. A hostler was making a two-team hitch to one of the husky freight wagons that weekly made the Elkton haul. The rhythmic ring of hammer on anvil sounded from the blacksmith's shanty at the lot's rear, where blue woodsmoke rose in a thin streamer from the forge chimney. Over by one of the open-fronted wagon sheds the carpenter was bolting a new axle onto a battered ore wagon that had its rear hoisted by a logging chain and block and tackle secured to a roof beam.

The office, flanked by a long loading platform running back into the yard, formed the far side of the gate. Danbo entered it by way of the street door, finding Bailey, the bookkeeper, across by the railing and cashier's cage that closed off the room's rear working space, talking to a tall, bearded man in buckskins. A saddle, bedroll, and booted Winchester lay on the floor at the stranger's feet.

Danbo was approaching the gate in the railing,

21

headed for the back office, when Bailey called to him. "Mr. Danbo, you better handle this."

Danbo had no sooner glanced at Bailey than his thinly veiled look of alarm warned him of something being wrong here. The next moment the stranger was looking at him and saying pleasantly, "I stopped in hoping to find Ned. Since he's away, I'd like the loan of a horse to get me out to the layout and . . ."

Pausing in mid-sentence, the tall man smiled sheepishly and hastened to explain, "Forgot to mention it, but the name's Speer, Will Speer."

For an instant Danbo wondered if the name should mean something. Then suddenly it did and he stood dumfounded, momentarily wondering if his hearing had deceived him. When he was sure it hadn't, a hard alertness crowded out his surprise. *Now what can this joker's game be?* he asked himself, at once positive that the stranger was lying.

Convinced that he had a brazen impostor on his hands, he nonetheless managed to say heartily, "Not Ned's partner!"

"The same." The stranger appeared relieved as he nodded to indicate Bailey. "Your friend here wasn't so sure about me. Maybe it's the beard." He laughed, reaching up to run a hand over his curly close-cropped whiskers.

"Now why the devil couldn't Ned be here?"

As he spoke, Danbo was thinking, *So he's a horse thief!* his quick mind weighing various ways of dealing with this situation.

22

Suddenly he thought of a way and, eyeing the bookkeeper, told him, "Bailey, get out and have Abe put a bridle on the bay for Speer. And while you're about it, tell Kelso and Worts to bring me those tally sheets."

For a moment he thought Bailey might spoil this, for there was no man by the name of Abe among the crew, and Kelso and Worts had nothing to do with tally sheets. He saw the book-keeper's brows arch briefly in puzzlement. But then to his vast relief the man gave him an owlish look of understanding and turned to leave the room by way of the platform door.

Danbo opened the gate in the railing now, went through it saying, "So you're Will Speer!" He chuckled, his glance taking in the stranger's high-built frame and the gun he wore along his thigh. "Ned's going to think he's seeing a ghost. How come you didn't let him know you were headed home?"

"Figured I'd make better time than a letter."

Danbo nodded. The stranger, looking slowly around the room, remarked, "At least this hasn't changed as much as the town. How's the yard doing?"

Danbo shrugged, deliberating for some seconds in his answer, for he wanted to kill time. "Pretty good, all in all. We do a steady business bringing in ore from the mines to the mill, then hauling the concentrates across to the railroad. But the stage end of the business is getting tricky. Been losing an express box now and then.

23

Lost a heavy one last week, in fact. We're lucky we haven't so far lost a man. Had one winged a while back, but he was back at work the following week."

The tall man's look had sobered. "Can't you hire a good shotgun rider?"

"Not for under fifty dollars on the run to Bend and Leesville. Which is why Ned's away. He's riding shotgun."

Danbo just then glimpsed two figures hurrying past the platform window, the sight bringing him a feeling of such keen relief that he turned away momentarily, afraid his expression might betray him.

The street door creaked open, and at that sound Danbo swung around to see burly Matt Kelso and Clyde Worts — who had never been known to unbelt his low-slung Colt's except when he went to bed — stepping into the room. Danbo couldn't hold back a thin smile then as the stranger glanced idly around at the two yard men.

"Boys," Danbo loudly announced, "want you to meet Ned's partner, Will Speer."

The stranger nodded to the two, his look gradually turning impassive when neither of them said anything. They were staring at him in such open hostility that Danbo knew the moment had arrived for a showdown.

"Friend, your luck's run out on you," he said tonelessly, hearing the door behind him open and shut as Bailey returned.

The tall man looked quickly around, strong puzzlement written on his dark face. "My luck? Afraid I don't get you."

Danbo was through pretending now and he swore softly, letting go the rein he had been holding on his temper. "Just how the hell could you play us for being such suckers? Because you knew Ned was away? Because you found out there isn't a man left in the yard that ever laid eyes on the real Will Speer? I'll have to hand it to you though. This is a slick try at stealing a horse."

The stranger's face had gone slack in such seemingly genuine surprise that Danbo told himself, *He should've been a gambler.* Then the stranger, with a baffled shake of the head, was saying, "You've got me wrong, dead wrong. I really am Will Speer. All you've got to do to prove it is —"

"All I've got to do to prove it is be able to read!" Danbo cut in curtly. "The paper had the story two months ago. About Will Speer being buried over on the reservation at Fort Lapwai. Along with thirty or forty other poor devils the cavalry lost in that ambush back in June."

"Then the paper had it wrong. I took a bullet through the shoulder, but —"

Danbo's patience was at an end. It was the curt nod he gave Worts that made the tall man check his words and, sensing that this was some sort of signal, wheel quickly around. By this time Worts's .44 was lined squarely at him.

25

"All right, Kelso," Danbo snapped. "You know what to do."

Kelso at once moved in on the stranger, circling so as to come in on his right side. He was smiling in a gloating way as he breathed, "Stay set, neighbor," and reached out to lift the tall man's gun from holster.

Suddenly then, in a wickedly fast move, he arced the weapon up and swung it at the stranger's head. Yet, fast as he moved, the tall man lunged back out of the way with catlike quickness, caught his down-swinging arm and with surprising ease twisted it sharply behind him.

Kelso cried out in agony as his arm was bent upward and the gun wrenched from his hand. His cry had barely died away when his solid bulk all at once hurtled across the ten feet separating him from Worts. He slammed into Worts, who stumbled, threw both arms about him and somehow managed to keep from falling. Worts had momentarily forgotten his .44. By the time he let go his hold on Kelso he found himself staring into the bore of the stranger's weapon.

Danbo, as Kelso cried out, had reached in under his coat to draw his flat double-barreled derringer from its shoulder holster. In a swift, sure lift of his arm he now reached out across the railing and jabbed the derringer hard against the back of the stranger's neck, saying with ominous softness, "Don't make me use this!"

For an instant he thought the stranger was

going to turn on him. But then he felt the tension go out of that high frame. The next moment the stranger's gun thudded to the floor.

"Now, boys, have your fun. Come get him!"

Caroline Knight spent forty minutes at the Emporium looking over the store's new shipment of drapery materials, choosing several yards of it and arranging to have it sent to Ruth Moore, the seamstress. Leaving the store she turned up Grant Street, deciding to walk rather than ride the short distance out to the Moore house so that she could give Ruth the measurements for the living-room windows.

Though modestly, even plainly dressed in contrast to some of the women along the street, there was an unconscious air of grace about Caroline Knight that set her apart from most others. Today her ebony hair was topped by a small and saucy square of maroon velvet edged with white braid. That bit of cloth, a token of her rebellion against the current fashion of large and ornate hats, was as typical of her as the light bronze tone of her skin in this day when women prided themselves on having fair complexions untainted by overlong acquaintance with the sun.

Had anyone told Caroline Knight that she was beautiful, she would have laughed outright; for she knew that her mouth was too wide for real prettiness, that her thick eyebrows marred the otherwise delicate makeup of her features. Nevertheless, there was as positive a quality of beauty about her as there was of high spirits, this last being quite evident in the lively and straightforward look of her dark brown eyes.

She was a girl possessing abundant vitality. And this, so evident to anyone glimpsing her tall and slender figure moving along the walk, made her the target for the interested and respectful glances of most of the men who passed her.

Half a minute after leaving the Emporium, she was glancing obliquely ahead across the street and soberly reading the new sign on the archway over the stage-lot gate. Hardly able to define why the sign displeased her, she told herself, *It's part of all the rest, Ned hasn't been himself lately, and I wonder why.*

The thought troubled her. She was thinking back to the time she had last seen Ned and remembering his high nervousness, when abruptly across the way she saw two men run from the stage-office door and one turn upon the other to hit him full in the chest.

The man who had struck the blow was Matt Kelso. The other, taller and wearing buckskins, now moved in at Kelso with surprising quickness, caught him about the waist and lifted him bodily from the walk to throw him out against the office tie-rail.

The rail snapped, broke with a crack she could hear quite plainly. And as Kelso fell awkwardly into the dust she saw men running along the walks and across the street to watch the fight.

This moment a third man lunged out of the office door to leap upon the tall man's back. The two of them staggered off the walk's edge, fell alongside Kelso and out of sight behind the gathering crowd.

Caroline hurried on along the walk, briefly glimpsing Kelso and the tall man through the fog of dust lifting across there. She saw the tall man's head suddenly drop from sight behind the onlookers. Then abruptly she could see him lying in the dust, and see Matt Kelso aim a solid kick at his chest.

It was over then. The crowd moved in and two men pulled Kelso away. A moment later Carry saw Lyle Danbo appear briefly in the office doorway to heave a saddle and bulky bedroll out onto the walk. Then Kelso and the man who had helped him in the fight went into the office and the crowd thinned and started breaking up.

She had stopped to watch all this, and now a man standing near her said to a companion, "Took two to do it. Good scrapper, whoever he is."

Carry's glance strayed back to the tall man. He was on his feet once again and had picked up his hat and was using it to beat the dust from his buckskin pants and shirt. She watched him step over and lift the saddle and bedroll to his shoulder. And suddenly she was staring at him incredulously, her eyes wide in outright bewilderment.

He had started on down the walk when an irresistible impulse made her turn and run out into the street, calling, "Will! Will, is it you?"

She saw him hesitate and turn to face her. The street became a blur and she realized that there were tears in her eyes. She ran on a few more steps, then abruptly slowed her stride as doubt struck her. For this man wore a beard, as Will never had. She was mistaken.

Yet this moment the tall man smiled broadly, eased the saddle down from his shoulder and laid it on the walk. He stepped off the edge of the planks and came toward her. And as suddenly as her doubt had come it was gone, and she started toward him again.

"Will, oh, Will! You aren't . . ."

She choked back her words as they met. She reached out and took him by the arms. She looked up into his blue eyes and was shocked and stirred to her depths by the tenderness and bridled longing she saw there.

He said gently, "Carry, I'm back."

It was the sound of his voice, its fullness and steadiness, that shook her and broke the dam of her restraint. She was trembling as she came into his arms. Unashamedly bursting into tears then, she kissed him full and hard on the mouth.

The Leesville stage was two hours late that afternoon, having been delayed by the tardy arrival of the narrow-gauge's noon local at the rail town.

Ned Oakes, on hearing the news of Will Speer,

was so incredulous that he threatened the man who first gave him the word. Then, finally convinced, he let out a delighted yell that rang half the length of Grant Street, afterward roaring, "Boys, watch out! This'll be a night to set the calendar by! Where is he?"

Amazed and delighted as he was, his exuberance lasted little better than an hour. It was as he and Will were eating their supper at the hotel that the first damper was clamped on his high spirits by Will asking about Danbo, about the new partnership, and finally about affairs at the stage yard.

At length he waved Will to silence. "We'll hash the whole thing out in the morning at the office. I'll get word to Danbo to be there. Now let's get caught up on things with you. What about the chunk of lead you stopped in that brush with the Nez Perces?"

As the evening wore on, as he and Will made the round of their old hangouts — the War Paint, Amos Soule's faro parlor, Daisy Kemp's Rosebud Lounge — Ned gradually sensed that this wasn't going to be a night to mark on the calendar after all. Except, of course, that he'd always remember it as the day Will Speer returned from the dead.

That same feeling of old, of respect and liking and complete trust, still lay between them, based as it was on eleven years' close acquaintance. But as the hour grew later Ned became increasingly restless and uneasy in the presence of this

31

tall and quiet-spoken man who seemed in so many ways so much older than he, though there wasn't a year's spread between them. The past twenty-three months had brought a maturity on Will, a surprising one in spite of his always having been the more serious of the two.

There were things that had happened during Will's absence, particularly during the past few weeks, that Ned would never be able to explain to his friend. Half ashamed of this, half angered by it, Ned drank far more heavily than his partner who seemed to be able to make a glass last a full hour.

Finally they found themselves in Ned's upstairs room at the back of the hotel, an open bottle on the table. They got to talking about the old days, about Crow Track and the homestead, and most of Ned's uneasiness ebbed away. Presently he left the table and lay back on the bed, a glass in hand, and began expounding on something that forever afterward remained a mystery to him, though later on he did distinctly remember having closed his eyes as he talked.

He wakened with a start to find the room's lamp turned low and Will gone. He looked at his watch. It was ten minutes past midnight. Suddenly he thought of something that sobered him to an alarming degree. He quickly left the room, went down the stairs and out onto the street, turning up along it toward Lupin Street and Lyle Danbo's house.

Walking fast, the night's chill air ridding his

brain of its fuzziness, he found himself thinking back and remembering things he had come close to forgetting for a long, long time.

The picture that stood out clearest of all in his mind was of a summer day, close to ten years ago, when he and Will had returned to the wagon camp after a long day's fruitless hunt for game. The smell of the charred wagons and the look of the sprawled bodies came back to him tonight as sharp and clear as though it had been only yesterday or this afternoon.

After dusk that evening, he remembered, two other survivors of the party, grown men, had come out of the pine forest to join them. The four had buried their dead in the dark; his mother and father, Will's father and sister with the rest. They had been long gone from the spot by dawn the next morning, two sixteen-year-old boys turned men in a twelve-hour span of time.

Traveling only by night, they had struck north for the Missouri. Five long rides had brought them quite by chance to Crow Track, Tom Knight's new ranch. Knight had offered them good wages and safety. They had worked on the layout for four years, until the country quieted down under one of the many uneasy truces with the hostiles. Then they had struck out on their own, mainly at Will's insistence, and homesteaded a choice piece of land between Crow Track and the river where lay the new-built settlement of Rock Point.

They had been close as brothers throughout

those years, closer perhaps because they lacked the blood tie that so often creates friction and envy. Even now Ned could honestly tell himself that he would do more for Will Speer than for any other man alive. A part of him that had withered two months ago on reading of Will's death had come alive tonight.

But with that part of him made whole once again, a host of troubled thoughts, of uncertainties, had come alive, too. Which was why he was on his way to see Lyle Danbo at this midnight hour.

Albert, Danbo's ageing Negro servant, let him in the door and showed him into the small sitting room across the hallway from the big parlor where the click of chips told him the nightly game was in full swing. He began restlessly pacing the broad window alcove overlooking the night-shrouded street. Less than a minute later, on hearing the hallway door open, he wheeled around.

Worry was plainly written on his slender and handsome face as, without preliminary, he asked, "Lyle, what do we do now?"

Danbo was smoking a thin cheroot and didn't answer until he had reached up and taken it from his mouth. "You've seen him then?"

"Spent the evening with him," Ned answered, nodding nervously. "And don't ask if I gave anything away because I didn't."

"Wouldn't hurt anyone but you if you had." Danbo's smile was thin, distant. "So you patted him on the back, told him the greatest thing that ever happened was finding out he was still alive. You bought him drinks and supper. You said, 'Now, Will, let's wait till tomorrow to talk business. Danbo's easy to get on with and we'll straighten this whole thing out in five minutes. Nothing to worry about at all.' " Pausing momentarily, Danbo asked, "Is that about how it went?"

"Just about," Ned admitted. He couldn't overlook the other's heavy sarcasm, and added, "Quit pushin' at me. I'll take just so much!"

Danbo shrugged, turning away to grind out his half-finished smoke in a tray on the marble-topped center table. "All right, Ned, this is for you to figure out. Since you're the one that's in the bad spot."

Ned sighed gustily, his habitual lightheartedness having deserted him completely. He lifted a hand and ran it across his wavy, ash-blond hair, afterward saying, "One thing's got to be understood. Will's never to know the truth about our deal. The same as you agreed Carry never would."

"Know the truth about what?" Danbo asked blandly. "It slips my mind."

"It damn well better not! He's not to know why you put up the five thousand to buy a partnership in the yard."

"But I did put up the five."

"In a way you did, yes. But —"

"In a way?" Danbo echoed dryly. "Those slips of paper we burned had your name on 'em. You owed the five, didn't you?"

"Money I lost at that confounded table across there." Ned gestured angrily in the direction of the hallway.

"Don't blame your luck at cards on me, my friend." The gambler peered intently at Ned a moment trying to decide if too much drink was responsible for the man being so high-strung and testy. In the end he decided it wasn't, and said, "You blame me because you lost. So suppose I take credit for the last two times you sat in the game. You packed away a fair chunk of cash each time."

"Is eight hundred dollars big money?"

Abruptly Ned's ill-humored expression softened, to be replaced by a look of contriteness. "What the devil, man! Let's quit clawin' at each other and get our heads together on what we're going to do about this."

"Let's," Danbo agreed readily enough. A thought just then made him chuckle softly. "You should've been there to see it. He handled Kelso like he would've a youngster. Your bearded friend can take care of himself."

"I missed the beard. Carry had made him shave it off and shed his buckskins by the time I met him. She and Tom told me about it, though, said he looked like something straight down out of a cave in the hills.

"He did, for a fact. Which is why I couldn't begin to believe his story. When do we get together with him?"

"In the morning at the office."

"Ought to be interesting," Danbo remarked wryly.

"Don't worry, Will never bears a grudge." Thrusting hands deep in pockets, Ned stared worriedly at the flowered carpet before looking up to ask, "Lyle, will you take my note for that five thousand again and call it quits on the partnership?"

Danbo's only answer was a smug smile, whereupon Ned asked in a pleading way, "If you don't, then what'm I to do? For God's sake think of something."

Once again Danbo eyed the blond man speculatively. This time a look of guile tinged his glance, and he said shortly, "Stay set. I'll be right back," and left the room.

He was gone less than a minute, during which time Ned resumed his pacing of the window alcove, presently pulling aside the lace curtains so as to draw the shades. Danbo appeared as the last blind was being drawn and nodded his approval, saying pointedly, "I was going to suggest we do that."

His words carried a meaning that escaped Ned, who asked, "Why?"

For his answer, Danbo reached into a pocket of his coat, drew out a fat leather bag the size of his fist and tossed it on the table. Ned, frowning, came across and picked up the bag, his eyes coming wider open as he hefted it.

He took in the crude outline of a bird burned

in the leather. Outrage tinged his glance then as it whipped across to the gambler. "Gold!" he breathed. "This is an Oriole bag."

"So it is."

Ned was staring at the man incredulously. "That box of Red Byrd's we lost last week! This came out of it."

Danbo only shrugged, whereupon Ned brandished the pouch close in front of his face, asking hoarsely, "You rigged that steal?"

Danbo's tone sounded almost hurt as he blandly answered, "Now let's don't go off half-cocked, friend. You've seen Red Byrd pay his poker losses here in gold. You've seen him hand me one of these pouches more than once."

Suddenly Ned's free hand stabbed out and caught a tight hold on the other's coat front. "By God, Lyle, last week you and I and Red and the bank were the only ones that knew the box was aboard that stage! You knew the other times, too. You've known what our rigs were carrying every damn time they've been stopped!"

Lyle Danbo nodded sparely. Yet there was an unmistakable intentness in the look he gave Ned as he said, "And if I backed out of the partnership I wouldn't know from now on, would I?"

His words carried a deeper meaning than Ned at first realized. Then, as Ned abruptly became aware of exactly what he was hearing, the gambler lifted a hand and almost gently broke his grip, saying quite casually, "By the way, how's the little widow across in Leesville? Did you happen to drop in on her again last night?"

Ned Oakes that moment had the appearance of a man all at once feeling violently ill. His face lost its healthy amber hue and took on a sickly pallor. His eyes mirrored naked fear. And his voice was hollow, without life, as he asked, "How . . . You've known it how long?"

"Does it matter how long?" Danbo lifted his hands outward from his sides in a mocking gesture of humility. "Now, Ned, I'm enough of a man to understand your liking the looks of a pretty woman. Especially as good a looker as Grace Drew."

"If Carry should ever —"

"Carry never will," Danbo cut in, his tone silky soft. "Not from me, she won't. Not unless it's by a slip. Or . . ."

As the man's words trailed off, a look of loathing briefly hardened Ned's expression. But then the starch went out of him and he reached up to run a hand across his eyes, afterward muttering lifelessly, "Carry never will know. Or Will either. Because there'll never be a reason for your telling them. So what is it you want me to do?"

TWO

Last night on his ride out to the homestead after leaving Ned Oakes asleep in his room at the hotel, Will Speer had noticed that the stars off to the east were obscured by a low bank of clouds. This morning towering thunderheads lay massed high above that horizon and there was a heaviness, a sultriness in the air that could mean nothing but a storm in the making.

He was in the saddle early, shortly after sunup, having cooked his breakfast in the one-room cabin he and Ned had shared when they first settled on this lush range. It had given him a twinge to find the cabin in such a state of disrepair, with one of its windows broken and much evidence of pack rats having taken over, and he was glad to leave the place for a swing across the creek meadow and the range to the south.

In spite of the gray, cheerless day, a keen exhilaration lifted in him once he was out of sight of the layout, his eye feasting hungrily upon the familiar vista of broken ridge and open grassland with here and there stands of lodgepole pine darkening the higher hill crests. His first leisurely hour of travel took him as far as the rocky escarpment of Buckhorn Ridge, a four-hundred-foot-high buttress that formed a natural boundary between his and Ned's range and that of Crow Track. Tom Knight's vast holdings ran on southward a good ten miles and stretched from east to west for double that distance.

It was as he turned back and began thinking of Caroline Knight, and of his visit with Ned last evening, that his feeling of release and contentment slowly left him to be replaced by a growing unease over certain subtle and seemingly unrelated facts he had come upon since yesterday's fight on the street. Standing out over all the others was an odd and nagging conviction that Ned's welcome had lacked a certain heartiness toward the end of their mild celebration last night.

Yet it was typical of him that he didn't brood over-long on these imponderables, that he closed his mind to them and decided to suspend judgment until he had more than his own speculation to rely upon.

But one thing he was seeing here and now did puzzle him so strongly that he couldn't ignore it. Since leaving the cabin he had seen only eight or ten scattered bunches of cattle, the largest numbering no more than twenty animals. When he had left here two years ago he and Ned had counted upward of five hundred head in their herd. From what he had seen this morning, he judged there couldn't be more than a quarter that number on their range now.

At first, as his curiosity mounted, he suspected that poor grass and a dry summer might be the answer. But the grass seemed plentiful, growing knee-high in the broad swales and coulees. The creek was running high for this time of year and the half dozen springs he came upon were flowing as well as at any time he could recall.

Here was a puzzle that confounded and worried him, and this was his mood as he came within sight of the corrals and outbuildings, the lone cottonwood and the cabin.

He at once noticed smoke drifting lazily groundward from the cabin chimney and wondered idly who might have stopped by to build up the fire in the stove during his absence. Some minutes later he made out a bay horse standing hipshot at the rail near the well, and his somber thoughts lightened somewhat at the hope that Ned had ridden out for a talk with him.

Closer in, he made out a figure standing in the cabin's doorway. Then in another minute, all at once recognizing who this was, he was once more feeling that inner warmth and gladness at being home again. He touched the claybank with spur and ran on in at the lope.

Caroline Knight stepped out of the doorway as he put the gelding alongside her Crow Track bay at the rail. He was surprised at seeing her carrying a broom and wearing a piece of flour sacking tied about her head. But otherwise she was as he had so long remembered her, wearing a pair of waist overalls, brown flannel shirt, and scuffed boots.

Recalling how he had yesterday been so awed by the changes in this girl, by her femininity and

42

striking womanliness, he smiled broadly as he came up to her, drawling, "This is more like it. You've shed the fancy duds."

"As I do every chance I get."

She tilted her head and airily regarded him a moment, a mischievousness in her glance. "Now I sort of wish you'd kept the beard, Will. It made you almost handsome."

He removed his hat and, with an exaggerated flourish, held it across his chest, bowing slightly. "Appreciate the compliment, ma'am. I'll grow a new one right away."

"A long one this time." She burst out laughing, the rich mellowness of her voice stirring him, bringing back memories he had so long tried to erase from mind. Then she was asking, "Care for coffee?"

"Lots of it." He pointedly eyed her improvised headgear. "Is that something special you ordered in from Omaha? And why the broom?"

"Come see."

She led the way back to the cabin. He followed her in through the doorway, halting sharply as his glance roved the room. Its scarred floorboards were swept clean; shreds of paper and rags that had earlier littered the far corner were gone; and wood was stacked neatly against the log wall behind the stove. The bunk he had slept in last night, one of a pair along the west wall, was made up, his blanket smooth and in place. Last of all, the big graniteware coffeepot simmered at the back of the stove to fill the room with a rich aroma.

Surprised and pleased, he nonetheless schooled his expression to one of strong annoyance, dryly saying, "Leave it to a woman to shuffle things around. A bachelor stands no chance at all. Now where'm I to find my tobacco? And what happens when I need a clean pair of socks or a shirt?"

She wouldn't be taken in by his baiting and archly replied, "A man has a hard time finding anything even when it's right under his nose. So what does it matter where I've put things?" She nodded to indicate the broken window. "You'll have to fix that, though. Why would Ned let the place go like this, even if he has moved to town? It wasn't fit for chickens. About the only time anyone's ever here any more is when the haying crew moves in."

Will shrugged. "Nothing's wrong that an hour or two's work won't fix now, thanks to you. You shouldn't have bothered, Carry."

"Why not? It was a way to kill time while I waited."

For some indefinable reason the girl's high spirits seemed subtly to have been dampened during this interchange, for her expression was unnaturally sober as she went to the stove corner, took two chipped china mugs down from the near-by shelf and filled them with coffee. Offering Will one, she told him, "I couldn't find a can of milk. But there's sugar in that jar."

"Don't use either, thanks."

Her glance showed a trace of startlement. "Now how could I have forgotten that? Of course you don't."

She came on past him then and crossed the room to sit on the foot of his bunk, setting her coffee on the floor and reaching up to remove her makeshift turban, afterward lifting both arms to tighten the ribbon that held her rich black hair in place at the nape of her neck.

That moment she made a graceful and striking picture, one to arrest a man's attention; her expression warm and alive, the firm roundness of her upper body shaping delicate lines above her narrow waist. And now Will was feeling a stir of that same strong emotion that had gripped him yesterday on the street when she had so impulsively and unexpectedly come into his arms and kissed him.

It suddenly struck him that he had been very mistaken yesterday morning, there on the *Belle*, in being so positive that his two-year absence had given him the strength of will to ignore the countless ways in which this girl attracted him. It hadn't, for over these past two minutes he had been keenly alert to her every change of expression, her every move. And this wasn't as he had planned it should be.

He wondered just now how much Carry might have guessed of his real reasons for leaving Rock Point two years ago, wondered if she even remotely suspected how intolerable he had found it to be such a constant witness to Ned Oakes's offhand acceptance of the affection she so generously gave the man. He supposed. he hoped, that Ned had come to realize how fortunate he was, though last night Ned had given him no inkling at all of how things stood with Carry these days.

"You're miles from here, Will. Care to take me along?"

The sound of her voice prodded him out of his indrawn mood, made him smile guiltily. Before he could think of an answer, she was speaking again, this time dryly, her words faintly edged with sarcasm. "Is your foot beginning to itch already? How long will it be before you pull up stakes and drift again? A day, a week, a month?"

"Hadn't thought much about it, Carry." The barbs in her questions stung. He couldn't begin to understand what had so roused her.

She had been eyeing him speculatively, and now mused, "I can remember summer before last so clearly. How strange you were. How I asked Ned about it, and his telling me he couldn't understand it either. Then finally how you told us one day you were leaving to hire on as a cavalry scout. You and Ned had a few scalps coming to you, you said. And you weren't coming back till you'd collected them."

"Which was the truth," he put in uneasily.

"Part of the truth maybe, but not all of it, Will. When I . . . When we heard you'd been killed, I remember thinking, 'The fool! The poor sweet fool. Now I'll never know what he was running

46

from.' And to this day I don't."

"Running from?" He forced a laugh he sensed was far from convincing. "Carry, you're dreamin'."

"Was it a girl . . . a woman?"

This time his laugh was wholly genuine. Carry, ignoring it, insisted, "Then why did you leave? You weren't so all-fired sore at the Cheyenne and the Sioux that you had to drop everything and go off to join the fighting. If you really felt that way you'd have done it long, long ago."

She was skirting the edges of something he had no intention of getting involved in, and he drawled, "There's no telling why a man does what he does. Or a woman either. So suppose we forget it."

"Forget it? How can I?" She was eyeing him intently, as though trying to decide something about him. "I don't always think too hard when I put together my prayers. But last night was different, Will. I gave thanks for your being alive, first of all. And then I prayed that you wouldn't leave us again."

He was embarrassed and felt his face go hot. Carry evidently didn't notice, didn't expect him to say anything, for abruptly her eyes mirrored a strong impatience as she asked bluntly, "Don't you think it's time you stopped drifting and took on some responsibility?"

"Depends on what you mean by 'responsibility,' " he warily answered.

"I mean what you owe Ned. Nothing more.

Would it mean anything to you to know that your leaving nearly ruined him?"

There was a very real animosity in her this moment, one she had never before shown him. And as he stood speechless, she said hotly, "Look at the spot he's worked himself into. Taking on a gambler as a partner."

"I'd wondered how that came about."

"You'd wondered." She rose up off the bed now, speaking in a voice roughened by a very real indignation, "Well, so have Tom and I wondered how it came about. But as for you, do you really care anything at all about Ned any more? Or about me?"

He shook his head in honest bafflement. "Girl, just what the devil did I do or say to bring this on?"

"It's what you didn't do, leaving Ned on his own."

"He's done fine on his own. I told him last night it was hard to believe what he's made of the yard." He eyed her questioningly, wondering what she was driving at. "Besides, the boy's over twenty-one. Why can't he look out for himself without a —"

"Why?" she cut in. "Because he's had enough bad luck lately to last a man half a lifetime."

"Such as what?" he quietly asked.

"Such as one of his drivers losing a brand-new coach three months ago in a washout during a storm up Two Mile. Along with two fine teams. Then a week later a man named Drew at the yard in Leesville got drunk, tipped over a lantern and set the barn afire. Drew died in the fire. He left a widow Ned's having to look after. And with all that, it wasn't another week before the word reached us about your being scalped and buried."

"Ned mentioned the fire last night, mentioned this man that got caught in it. But he didn't say anything about the widow."

"He wouldn't. Not last night at any rate. You two were supposed to be enjoying yourselves." She paused to regard him aloofly, almost with distaste. "Is it any wonder that the bank, that Tom and Baker couldn't risk making him a loan? And is it any wonder he'd go to a man like Danbo for money to keep the business going?"

"Maybe not," he admitted. "But didn't he say he'd had the cash on hand to build the new barn?"

"Yes. Money he got by selling cattle off the layout here."

"Why didn't he use the cash he'd banked for me?"

"Because you weren't here to tell him he could."

She walked to the door now, glanced briefly outside, then turned to put her back to the wall and regard him once more with that same thinly veiled anger showing in her dark eyes. "I don't say that none of this would have happened if you'd been here. But it might not. If you had been here you might have been driving the day that stage was lost up Two Mile. You might have saved it. And you might have been driving last week when that gold shipment was lost. Did Ned tell you about that?"

"Yes. No particulars, though." She had been roughing him with her tongue, yet there was no resentment whatsoever in him as he asked, "Just what is it you want me to do, Carry?"

"It's not what I want. It's what I'd like you to want to do."

"And what's that?"

"Go in there this morning and tell Danbo he's through as Ned's partner. If he's lent Ned money, tell him you'll arrange for a loan at the bank and pay him back; call it quits with him. Tom and Baker will listen to you and Ned now that you're back."

He carefully weighed what she had said as he sipped the last of his coffee. These past few minutes had shown him something he was powerfully aware of this moment: that his long absence hadn't loosened the bonds that attracted him to this girl. To stay on here and be around Caroline Knight even rarely would only deepen the unease he was feeling right now. Carry belonged to Ned Oakes. He was willing to face that and accept it. But he wasn't willing to face the day in and day out awareness that he must never betray his feelings toward her.

Now was the time to make a clean break, to settle this once and for all. He'd had that intuition yesterday and last night, though he hadn't consciously recognized it.

He could wind up his affairs here in three or four more days at the outside. Then he was leaving, leaving for good.

That decided, he looked at Carry, drawling, "It wouldn't work. You say you've wondered why I left here two years ago. Well, half the reason was that I was a third wheel on the cart. The yard just wouldn't bring in enough for the both of us once Ned took himself a wife."

Her eyes came wider open in surprise, and she said quickly, "You're so wrong, Will. This boom hadn't even started back when you pulled out. Right now Ned could do twice the business they're doing if he only had someone he could depend on to help him. And Lyle Danbo can't be any help there, none at all."

Will shook his head dubiously, whereupon she insisted, "I know what I'm saying. But there's something else, a stronger reason for your staying. Ned and I have never talked about it, but I can feel things aren't going right for him. He . . . it isn't often he laughs the way he used to. It's almost as though he's hiding something. Or that he's afraid. He needs you, Will."

An irrational anger all at once mounted in Will, and he said tartly, "You're the one he needs. You're two plain fools for having waited. You should've grabbed that man two years ago and led him to the church. If you had, he'd still be the same."

She smiled faintly, amused at his sudden vehemence. But then her expression gradually sobered as she considered some strictly private thought. At length she came across and set her cup on the table, telling him, "A woman knows when things are right and when they aren't, Will. Things haven't been right with Ned and me. I want them to be. You're part of it."

"I don't get that at all."

Her glance touched him briefly in a way that was almost shy and she murmured, "No, I don't suppose you do."

Something subtly intimate lay between them now, a thing indefinable but nonetheless real. He knew that she sensed this as keenly as he, for she hastened to say, "All right, I'm a poor persuader. So we'll forget you and just plain hope Ned can stumble onto a way of straightening things out." She folded her arms across her breasts, staring at him very soberly. "How soon will you be leaving?"

Her question made him squirm inwardly. She had managed to put him at a strong disadvantage, managed to make him appear selfish even in his own eyes. Until scant moments ago he had made himself look upon this matter callously, ignoring all sentiment as he countered her every argument in favor of his staying.

But now he knew that it wasn't in him to turn his back upon her or upon Ned. It was that positive. In thirty seconds' time this girl had made him completely reverse his way of thinking.

Reluctantly, knowing he might regret his

change of mind even before the day was out, he asked, "Just what is *it* you'd have me do, Carry?"

Her eyes lighted up with a radiance that shook him. "You mean . . . You mean you'll listen after all?"

"Looks like I'll have to. What do I do?"

That moment her glance was eloquent, warmly and tenderly speaking her thanks. "Just as I was saying. Go in there and see Ned and Danbo. Tell Danbo you're Ned's partner and he isn't. Don't back down to a thing. Buy him out."

He breathed a deep sigh, a broad grin slowly softening the stern set of his angular dark face. With a baffled shake of the head, he drawled, "First time I ever thought you might be the kind to put a ring in a man's nose once you had him."

"You bet I might be!"

She laughed, and now it was as it had always been between them. They were lightheartedly sparring with their words, masking their strong awareness of the bond of trust and affection that lay between them.

Ned Oakes had spoken only briefly throughout this ten-minute interval the three of them had been in the stage office. He was letting Danbo and Will do the talking, not quite trusting himself to explain the details he and Danbo had agreed upon last night.

Just now the gambler abruptly rose from the chair behind the desk, stating, "It's settled. My hat's about the only thing I brought with me to

53

this place. So I put it on and clear out for good."

Will Speer's only visible reaction to this blunt announcement was a slight shifting of his wide shoulders to put them more squarely against the deal filing cabinet at the room's inner corner. And Ned, knowing him as well as he did, sensed that his friend's lazy stance and easy-going manner over these past few minutes had hidden a strong surprise and perhaps a measure of suspicion at Danbo's startling pronouncement that he was ready and willing to call it quits on his partnership. It was obvious that Will had come here expecting a far different reaction from the man.

"Seems like you ought to be getting something out of this, Danbo," Will said now. "After all, you put in close to two months' time here. And you put up five thousand dollars of your money."

"Time?" Danbo glanced at Ned. "Ask Ned how much I've put in. Practically none at all. This was a handy place to loaf a couple times a week, nothing more. As to the money, we've already told you not a cent of the five thousand was spent. I've only kept it handy in case it was needed, which it wasn't. Right, Ned?"

Ned tilted his head in the affirmative, warily wondering if Will was convinced. "He's right, Will. Things I'd expected to happen just plain didn't. Like building the new Leesville stable. The market for beef went up, I made a nice profit selling off our herd, or most of it. So I didn't need the cash Lyle had ready and waiting."

"Lucky all the way around, eh?" The gambler, closely eyeing Will, went on, "That's the way it happened, Speer. Ned had had a damn poor run of luck, it looked like he needed money. Is it any wonder he took me up on my offer, the paper saying what it had about you?"

"No wonder at all," Will agreed.

"Then it shouldn't surprise anyone that I'm pulling my stake out and leaving you partners like you were. No one's any the worse off" — Danbo chuckled softly — "except for Matt Kelso. You connected with a nice one out there yesterday. Matt's seeing out of only one eye this morning. No hard feelings about that, are there?"

"Not any." Will smiled, shaking his head. "You must've taken me for a real brush jumper. If it had been the other way around I'd have tossed you out."

"And not with half the trouble you gave us."

Danbo came from behind the desk now, crossing the small room to the inner door. Ned, watching him, thought, *He made it sound good, just right.* Then in another moment the gambler, opening the door, looked around at Will to say, "Stop by at the house some evening if you feel the urge to try your luck at cards, Speer. Ned can tell you I run a reasonably honest game."

"Reasonably." Ned grinned, adding, "Thanks, Lyle. Be seeing you."

The door closed behind the gambler. And Will, sighing long and loudly, drawled, "This is hard to believe. We're lucky, friend. You especially."

"Why me?"

"For picking such a square shooter to throw in with."

"Would Ned Oakes pick any other kind?" Ned laughed. "He was damned white about the whole thing."

"Once every now and then you come across a gambler like that, a gentleman."

Will sauntered over to the platform window now, peering out across the lot. Ned, following his partner's glance, eyed the banners of dust blowing in through the gate and the ominous blackness of the sky above the rocky escarpment to the east.

"Two hours from now she'll be rainin' buckets," Ned remarked. "So the driver on the run to Bend and Leesville this afternoon'll be sitting the seat without me for company."

Will looked quickly around. "Didn't you say last night that the bank was sending a box across to Wells-Fargo today?"

"I did. But overnight old Baker got jumpy about it. This morning he sent a man out to bring Tom in and they had another confab. Tom stopped by just before you got here to tell me they'd called it off."

"What're they scared of?"

"Our losing that express box last week."

Will stared thoughtfully out across the yard once more. Ned, watching him, gave way to a sudden impulse and reached out to shake him by the shoulder, saying heartily, "Can't get over you being back, you lanky devil. Now thing's'll begin to roll around here."

"Beginning today, I hope." Will eyed his partner with a frown. "Let's get up to the bank and try changing Baker's mind. If we can, then you and I can take the haul to Bend and Leesville. Like in the old days, unless I've forgotten how to handle the ribbons."

Ned let his hand fall away, a tightness of apprehension gathering in him. "What's the difference who drives? We still run the chance of being stopped." Sensing that his words sounded somehow inadequate, he went on urgently, "Believe it or not, but last week they even made a try at the driver. And you know damn well that throwing lead at a driver isn't the way even the tough ones play the game."

"What does Sheriff Hopps in Leesville say to all this?"

"Nothing he can say. He had a tracker out last week trying to follow the sign of the men that got away with the box. But he had no luck at all."

"Why couldn't Hopps have a deputy ride the gold hauls?"

"He's willing. But who'd foot the bill? We would. Besides, a man with a badge would give it away every time he rode shotgun."

Will turned impatiently away, striding across

to the inner door and putting his back against it. "Ned, this works two ways. By now the whole town probably knows the bank isn't shipping today. The weather'll be foul, which would help us if we can only get Baker and Tom to change their minds. If they do, I'll lay you ten to one we make Leesville without trouble."

This moment Ned was bleakly remembering last night, recalling Danbo's ultimatum that had been the price for giving up his partnership in the yard. It was this that made him insist, "But suppose we are stopped?"

Will regarded his partner in a probing, wondering way that only heightened Ned's uneasiness. "What's come over you? I can remember your tackling worse things than this at the drop of a hat."

Ned's glance fell away. "You haven't lived with this, Will. I have. I don't run those fool risks any more."

"Don't we make more out of hauling an express box than we do out of a full load of passengers?"

When Ned only nodded grudgingly in answer, Will asked, "You think someone's known when the gold was going out? Someone besides you and Danbo and the bank?"

"I'm sure of it."

"What about this crew you've got?" Will's tone was larded with irritation. "What's happened to Bill and Curly and Denver?"

"They quit. Claimed they could make better

wages up at the diggin's. The only man left of the old bunch is Prentiss across in Leesville."

"Why not pay what they ask and have 'em back again?"

Here was a ticklish point. Since his talk with Danbo last night Ned had several reasons for not wanting his old crew back again. Yet, knowing Will could knock holes in any argument he could think of, he said hesitantly, "Might be worth thinking about."

Will's vacant stare told Ned that his partner was abruptly thinking of something else. And in another moment the tall man was saying, "If the bank will play along, you and I can wait till the last minute and then say we're driving across to look over the Leesville yard and pay Prentiss a visit. We'll head out the usual way. Only after we make the turn out the head of Lupin Street, we swing back down the alley, pick up the box at the bank and go on. Now if we do it that way, how can any one here at the yard be any the wiser?"

Ned at this moment began to wonder if in arguing this further he would be giving Will cause to suspect him in any way. Last night's talk with Danbo had bred in him a stark and deep-seated dread of what might happen today, tomorrow, or weeks from now, whenever he passed the word to the gambler that a stage was carrying gold. That had been their agreement, arrived at after Danbo's shrewd, cold threat of blackmail.

Regardless of how long it might be postponed, Ned knew it to be inevitable that he would one day have to pay off his debt to the man. Meantime the fear that Will or Carry or Tom Knight might come to suspect him would haunt him as it had throughout the long, wakeful hours of last night after he left the house on Lupin Street.

His bleak realization of all this made him abruptly tell himself, *The hell with waiting! We'll get it over with.*

The thought no sooner struck him than he was feeling almost lightheaded with relief. If he and Will could convince the bank, and if the bank shipped a large enough amount today, then by night his worries might be over and he might be a free man once again.

So now he lifted his hands outward from his sides in a gesture of surrender. "You win. I'd forgotten how damn tight you get the bit in your teeth and never let go. Only I don't like any part of it, Will. Not any."

"You've got to like it. Either we lick this thing and figure some way of hauling the dust out of these diggin's or someone else will. When that happens we're whittled right down to the pint-sized outfit we were when we started."

"Which wasn't much," Ned grudgingly agreed.

"And take the bank," Will went on. "They can't shy away from this forever. Either they clear out their safe, or sooner or later run the risk of having it blown open some night. You think the hard cases around this town are going to let sixty or seventy thousand in gold lie around without making a grab for it?"

"Try and tell old man Baker that."

"Which is what I aim to do. Right now. And while I'm at it, you try and find Tom and bring him to the bank."

Ned's hesitant nod was a signal for Will to reach his hat down from the elkhorn wall rack and open the room's inner door. He went out the door saying, "See you at the bank."

Ned listened for the slam of the street door. When it came he stepped out on the loading platform, closing the door softly so as not to attract the attention of Bailey in the front office.

He glanced quickly around the wind-swept yard, a strong annoyance stirring in him when he didn't find even one man of the crew in sight. They were keeping under shelter, out of this blustery weather, a fact which slightly complicated the errand he was setting out on.

Nonetheless he walked on back to the bunkhouse and looked in, only to find it empty. The same was true of the harness shack. But then, his luck taking a turn for the better, he picked the feed shed for his next stop.

He found Matt Kelso inside. The man was cutting a piece of sheet tin to fit the bottom of one of the big empty grain bins, and he looked around as he heard the scrape of Ned's boots.

"You alone, Matt?"

"Just me and the mice, boss." Kelso leaned the sheet of tin against the bin.

"Then get, this," Ned breathed, barely audibly, his glance fixed warily upon the open door. "If Speer and I drive the Leesville run this afternoon, you're to get the word to Danbo."

Kelso's left eye was swollen shut. But his right one went narrow-lidded with a look of cunning as he silently nodded.

It had started raining shortly after one o'clock, about half an hour before Will carried a heavy black leather satchel out of the bank's alley door and handed it up to Ned, who sat the high seat of the Barlow-Sanderson coach.

By the time they reached the foot of Two Mile nearly an hour later, the upward hills were all but obscured by the filmy banners of a near cloud-burst; and Cat Creek, close below the road, was already booming with angry, muddy runoff.

Will Speer wasn't particularly minding the foul weather, the past two years having taught him how to ignore all but the most formidable discomforts. It seemed, in fact, that his blood ran warm with the near-forgotten tug of the leathers as the two teams slogged up the canyon road's steep grade. It was good to feel the lurching of the coach under him as it swayed against the thorough-braces, and now his voice betrayed a heady lightheartedness as he turned to glance at Ned and say loudly, "Throw over a hook and line and you might snag a trout."

Ned made a wry face, making it plain that his mood in no way matched his partner's. He sat with the double-barreled shotgun resting muzzle outward across his lap, hands stuffed up the sleeves of his slicker, shoulders hunched. Water dripped steadily from the trough of his wide hat, and Will, noticing that, laughed softly. "Three more hours and we come up for air. How does a man kill an evening these days in Leesville?"

"Same as ever." Will was puzzled by an odd furtive quality that briefly touched Ned's glance. "Eat at Irma's, stop by at Pringle's for a drink, then head for bed. The morning local's never on time, so a man can sleep late if he wants."

"Does the new barn have a bunk room?"

Ned's only answer was a spare nod. And Will, sensing that the man wasn't in the mood for further talk, lazily swung the whip to put the teams on at a faster trot.

In ten more minutes they were on the open bench at the head of the canyon, with a wide loop of the river in sight two miles to the north and downward. The road was keeping to a westerly direction as it skirted the river's bottomlands. In five more miles, after it met the river at the settlement of Bend, it would swing straight south into the Burnt Hills. This was the long road to Leesville, the distance being over twice that of the direct Rock Point-Leesville road; but a mail contract and the chance of picking up passengers at Bend made it the route the stages always traveled on the southward run.

Watching the rain-misted river, Will presently made out a white object along the far, timbered shore. He lifted the whip, pointing to it.

"There's the *Belle* with a wood crew at work. A two-day chore, the captain said."

Ned looked off there and surprised Will by stirring from his preoccupied mood to say, "I'll be riding her down the river in a few days along with Tom and Carry. Tom bought Laird's horse layout down near Elkton last year. He's made me a good offer on some mares and geldings, so the three of us are going down there to drive them back."

"Sounds like a good way to spend a couple weeks." Will was reminded of another thing, and went on, "Carry came across this morning and swept out the cabin."

"She did?" Ned smiled guiltily. "Bet she combed me over for letting the place run down the way I have."

Will shook his head. "Not at all." He eyed Ned impassively a moment. "Y'know, you two could do worse than move in there after the wedding. Add another room, plaster the walls, and it'd be as snug a place as you'd want."

"Hunh-uh. It's town for me. Besides, where would you hole up if we moved onto the layout?"

"Hadn't thought about that part of it." Pointedly then, Will asked, "When's the date?"

"For the wedding?" Ned shrugged nervously. "Carry hasn't said."

"Me, I'd make her say."

"Try and make that girl say anything before she's ready," Ned stated ruefully. "But don't think I haven't tried."

Will pretended surprise. He didn't want to say what he was thinking just then, but the words were out before he could stop them. "Nothing's wrong between you two, I hope?"

"Nothing a man can peg down. She just keeps saying she wants to wait till spring."

"Talk her out of it."

"I keep trying to."

They fell silent once more, and in another forty minutes made the mail stop at the post office in Bend, where they picked up a passenger to keep company with the lone man who had boarded the stage at the Rock Point yard. They harnessed fresh teams at Spence's ranch, three miles south of Bend, and from there on the road wound in among a series of low ridges and buttes in its climb in the Burnt Hills.

And it was as the grade grew gradually steeper that Ned quietly announced, "It could happen any time from here on."

Only then did Will fully realize how very real must be his partner's concern over the safety of the express satchel that sat between them on the footboard. Here was the reason for Ned being so uncommunicative, so seemingly out of sorts; and it was a relief to Will to conclude that nothing more than this was responsible for the man's long silences.

Ned's remark had made Will's glance come restlessly alert. He tirelessly scanned the slopes ahead, and once his frame stiffened suddenly at sight of a flash of movement in the brush a scant hundred yards above the road. But in a few more seconds he relaxed, watching a whitetail buck, and not a rider, bound on up the slope and out of sight.

Presently Ned pointed ahead to say, "Up there's where they got us last week. By that table rock."

Will peered on along the puddled wheel ruts, seeing through the fog of the rain a high granite shelf some fifty rods ahead. It was at once obvious that the huge outcropping made an ideal spot for an ambush, for the road ran within twenty feet of its sheer face and it was impossible to see what lay directly beyond.

"How many were there?" he asked.

"That held up the rig? Two. They waited along the far side. Caught the joker riding shotgun half asleep. According to Kelso, all he did was dump his gun and reach for sky. I fired him the next day."

"Kelso, you say. What did he do?"

"The only thing a driver ever does. Sat tight."

Will shook his head, dryly stating, "This one wouldn't."

"No, not you. But sittin' tight's the rule for a hired driver."

During this interchange, Will's glance had clung to the high rock shelf they were approaching. And now, abruptly deciding something, he hauled on the reins and swung the teams hard to the right and off the road.

Ned looked around at him, sharply asking,

"What's this?" and he answered, "Just playing it safe."

The ground to the west of the road and behind the rock shelf sloped gently upward for perhaps three hundred yards before it was dotted by a scattering of oak brush. Will put the teams up the slope as far as the margin of the brush, then swung them on a line to parallel the road. And as they came even with the big outcropping lying a good hundred yards below, he looked down there and said, "False alarm."

In two more minutes they were on the road again, the teams at a spanking trot. Will wondered why Ned had said nothing over this tense interval and finally decided that with the chill and the rain the man was just plain miserable. So was he getting a little cold and a little tired.

The light began fading before they had gone another mile, and presently, with a heavy grayness settling across the sodden land, Ned stirred on the seat, shivering against the raw chill, saying, "Time to light the lamps."

"Let's don't. We're nearly there."

Ned shrugged and settled back into his slouch, neither stirring nor speaking again until the winking lights of Leesville came up out of the wet blackness a good half-hour later. Then, unexpectedly, he rocked his slender frame hard against Will's, saying with surprising cheerfulness, "So we made it all in one piece! Which means you were right. I was spooked over nothing at all."

"After last week you had a right to be."

This, Will was thinking, sounded more like the Ned of the old days. He understood now that his puzzlement and concern over Ned's strange behavior throughout the afternoon had been wasted. The man had simply been very worried, and with good reason.

The wail of a train whistle sounded from the far end of town as the stage rolled up the single street. It was then that Ned announced, "We stop at the hotel first, then take the cross street as far as the alley alongside Wells-Fargo. You dump me there and wait in the alley while I walk up the street and get Charlie Woods to open the office."

They dropped their two passengers at the hotel, swung down the cross street, then into the pitch-blackness of a passageway alongside the brick Wells-Fargo office. Once the big coach lurched to a stop, Ned handed Will the shotgun and stepped down to the wheel-hub, pausing long enough to say, "Be back in two minutes," before walking on out to the street.

Will was beginning to feel the chill. He swung stiffly down into the mud, the tenderness of the wound in his shoulder making him wince as he lifted down the heavy satchel. It was so black back here that he had to reach out with an elbow and feel for the brick wall to guide him as he made his way back along it, trying to wade out of the deeper mud.

He was even with the lead team before he found firmer footing. And now he leaned the shotgun against the wall and reached down to set the satchel alongside it, afterward straightening to swing his arms and blow on his hands, working the chill out of his high frame. He hoped that Ned wouldn't be too long, for he was hungry, the very thought of a hot meal making his mouth water.

Suddenly from the blackness of the passageway close behind him there came a whisper of sound, as though some object was being pulled gently and carefully from the deep ooze.

An instant wariness turned him rigid. He was wheeling toward the sound when a crushing blow caught him on the side of the head.

A blaze of light flashed before his eyes. Pain stabbed down into his spine, his knees buckled and he lurched heavily against the wall. He fell face down and helpless into the mud, his senses reeling as he vaguely felt a heavy object fall across his back.

A hoarse voice, seemingly from very far away, grated softly, "He's down! Here it is!"

Feebly trying to cling to consciousness, Will realized what this meant. There were at least two men here. They were after the gold in the satchel.

He dug his hands into the mire and tried to push himself up on his knees, and couldn't. But he had moved slightly. And now the thing that lay across his back slid down against his hand. He closed his fingers about it, dazedly aware that he was gripping the stock of the shotgun.

It took all his strength to roll on his side, to get a better hold on the weapon's smooth, slippery stock. He heaved himself on an elbow and managed somehow to lift the gun and draw back its two hammers.

That moment he heard another sound from back along the passageway, the quick-cadenced sucking of a running man's boots churning against the mud.

He lined the shotgun at the sound and pulled both triggers.

The thunderous blast tore the gun from his hand. Blended with the explosion, there sounded a shrill agonized scream. The rosy flash of the powder charges lit the passageway momentarily, clearly outlining a man's shape falling crookedly sideways.

THREE

The dead man lay face down and half buried in the mire, for the stage's two teams had bolted and run over him, panicked by the shotgun blast.

He was Clyde Worts, the hostler from the Rock Point yard who had yesterday helped Matt Kelso throw Will Speer out of the stage office.

Ned Oakes, with the Wells-Fargo agent at his heels, had been the first man to run down the dark, muddy passageway after the shotgun explosion pounded up the street. He had found Will on his knees, weakly struggling to get to his feet, the empty shotgun lying near by.

As the crowd gathered someone had brought a lantern. By its light it was found that the bank's money satchel was gone and that the stage's two teams were standing in a tangle of harness heads-on to a slab fence lining the back alley's far side. And presently, after Worts's body had been hurriedly covered with a tarp, it was Will Speer himself who had taken the lantern and gone along the alley to find a brown gelding wearing his and Ned's Hacksaw brand tied to a downspout at the far corner of the Wells-Fargo building.

This was obviously the animal Worts had been riding, one borrowed from the Rock Point yard. From the maze of puddled tracks near by no one

71

could tell whether one or two men had been with Worts; though, as the formless indentations lined out south up the alley, it soon became apparent that two riders had made the getaway.

Will at first had argued in favor of taking Worts's animal and, with the help of the lantern, trying to track the pair. But then common sense, along with the steady drizzle and Sheriff Jim Hopps's persuasive powers, had finally convinced him that this would be an impossible chore.

Over the next half-hour, after the crowd moved down to the courthouse and stood milling along the hallway outside the sheriff's office, Ned Oakes had kept in the background, able to add little to Will's account of what had happened. Ned was still feeling the aftereffects of the hard shock he'd had on finding Will. Back there in the dark passageway, first glimpsing Will in the flare of a match, he had experienced a moment of blind rage and panic in thinking that Lyle Danbo had betrayed him, that Will must either be dying or seriously hurt.

He was still thinking of Danbo as he listened to Will and Hopps and the others talking in the office. For this had been a close thing, too close to stand alongside Danbo's solemn assurance of last night that, come what might, Will would be safe.

When the doctor arrived and began examining the gashed lump on his head, Will had bleakly remarked, "Never thought I'd live to shoot a man from behind, let alone with buckshot."

The sheriff, the doctor, and three or four others had at once protested, all speaking in chorus. And afterward it was Jim Hopps who dryly voiced the sentiments of everyone present. "From behind, frontwards or sideways, this bird needed killin'. So don't be so damned choosy about how you did it, Will. Besides, you fired at a sound."

Now, as Will and Ned walked up the street from the courthouse in the chill, steady drizzle — Will wearing his wide hat lopsided because of the hen's egg swelling at the side of his head — Ned looked up at his partner to drawl in genuine relief, "You're plenty lucky, friend. Worts meant to cash you in."

"It felt like it."

As they walked on toward the lights of Irma's restaurant, Will said, "Tell you what. We eat a meal and dry ourselves out. Then one of us had better take that gelding and head on back to get the word to Tom and Baker. Ought to be easy to make it by nine by taking the short road."

"Talk sense, man. You're not stirrin' tonight. It'll be me that heads back. Besides, you're needed at the inquest in the morning."

Will gave his partner a troubled, baffled look. "How do you figure this? Was Worts the one that had the hunch on what we were hauling across here today? Who were the two others with him? Was he one of the pair that stopped your stage last week? And were the two that sided him to-

73

night two more men from the yard?"

Ned laughed uneasily. "Whoa, boy! I'm no fortune-teller. But there's one thing I am damn pleased with. That hunch you had this morning."

"Which was that?"

"The one that made you cut in half what the bank wanted to send across. Tom was all set there to make it thirty thousand, if you remember."

Will nodded, saying gravely, "This puts the bank in a rough spot, Tom along with it. And us, too."

"How come Tom and us?"

"Tom's part owner of the bank. He's liable for a share of any loss. And didn't he say this morning that they have eighty thousand more to go out, with more piling up every day?"

"So he did. But how does that ring us in on the thing?"

"We lose if we can't get their shipments out safely. We don't get paid a dollar for the haul we made today."

They strode on for several moments in moody silence before Will abruptly said, "I can't help thinkin' about Kelso."

Ned's nerves came instantly taut. "What about Kelso?"

"He helped Worts invite me off the premises yesterday. And this morning I noticed the two of them working in the corral together. Did they hang around together much?"

"Not that I ever noticed," Ned glibly lied.

"Even so, it wouldn't hurt to ask around when you get back tonight. If Kelso's there, try to find out where he spent the late afternoon. If he isn't, see if anyone saw him. Get it pegged down that he wasn't around town and we may have something to work on."

"We may," Ned stated dryly. "But if Matt Kelso was in on this we've seen the last of him. He might've risked coming back to his job if they'd made a clean getaway. But with what happened to Worts he's probably halfway to the Territory line by now."

Will sighed gustily in angry bafflement. "Then there's this. If he was one of the pair that got away, who was the other man?"

Ned reached out and laid a hand on the shoulder of his friend's wet slicker. "Take it easy, Will. All we're talkin' about is 'if' this and 'if' that. Let's think about food for a change. After we eat I'll head on back and see what I can turn up. That suit you?"

"It'll have to."

Some forty minutes later Ned rode out of the new barn's runway astride the gelding Worts had ridden. The prospect of two hours in the saddle — taking the short road across to Rock Point rather than the long one by way of Bend — wasn't much to his liking. But there were compensations. He had borrowed a sheepskin from Prentiss to wear under his slicker, his meal had warmed him. Best of all it was a keen relief to be

75

away from Will. For it had been a strain to be so constantly on his guard, knowing as he had since early afternoon that trouble might be in the offing.

When that trouble had come he had been caught completely by surprise. He hadn't for a moment thought that Danbo would have the audacity to stage a holdup in the heart of Leesville. Here, if he needed it, was further proof of the man's shrewdness and cunning.

It now abruptly occurred to him that he was wasting his time in mulling over what had happened tonight. His debt to Danbo was settled, he had paid it in full. From now on he was free, he could look Will Speer straight in the eye and not flinch inwardly as he had ever since their first meeting yesterday. As to Kelso, who must surely have been one of the two men siding Clyde Worts tonight, he was positive that he and Rock Point had seen the last of the man. For Worts's death would surely make Kelso's return to his job at the stage yard too risky a thing to be thought of.

His spirits soared as he reasoned all this out. For the first time in weeks his conscience was at ease, or practically so. He regretted Will's having taken so much punishment tonight, but consoled himself with the thought that another day or so would see his partner as fit as ever.

When he came abreast the small single-story house with the gingerbread trim on its porch and the lamplight shining so cheerily from its one front window, he had every intention of riding straight on. This he did, but for a distance of only a few rods. Then, unable to resist the pull of long habit, he abruptly tightened rein and turned about.

He rode back past the house and shortly swung off the dark street to angle across the vacant lot he knew so well. In another half minute he was knocking softly on the rear door of Grace Drew's house.

So it was that he didn't leave Leesville until well past eight o'clock.

The blast of the shotgun pounding out the foot of the passageway had tightened Lyle Danbo's slight frame in instant alarm. Stark fear had clawed at him as he took in the jingle of harness chains and the snorting of the panicked stage teams blindly milling about in the alley above.

He had tried to saw his horse around and clear of the other two, but the brute he was riding was hard-jawed and had only slammed hard against Worts's gelding, pinning his left leg. By the time he was clear of Worts's animal, he had heard someone slogging toward him through the mud. He had been sitting with gun in hand, and he lifted the weapon and lined it at the sound, tight-reining his fractious animal.

Then a moment later he lowered the weapon as Kelso's hoarse whisper sounded out of the blackness close at hand. "God A'mighty, they got Clyde!"

"Did you get what you went after?" Danbo's tone was curt, clipped.

"Here, take the damn thing!"

Danbo had felt a heavy object strike his thigh, and he reached down and took the satchel. He said, "Hurry it!" and turned his horse out into the alley, hearing a creaking of leather behind him as Kelso hurriedly heaved his heavy bulk into the saddle.

They went down the alley at a slow, cautious jog. When they had passed the last house, Danbo slowed to let Kelso come abreast him, saying, "You better lead the way," for the country around Leesville was unfamiliar to him.

They covered the better part of five hard miles before Danbo abruptly called out, "Far enough. Now pick us a spot where we can have some light."

Kelso swung sharply left down a brushy slope and led the way into a grove of dripping thinleaf cottonwoods, where he reined in to announce, "We're three miles from the road and not a house within another mile. Now what's on your mind with this light?"

"Want to give you your share, Matt."

"Can't we do that later?"

"No. Leaving Clyde back there changes a few things."

"What way?"

"If Speer . . . What happened to Speer, by the way?"

"Clyde had to slug him. I could see by the light

78

off the street. If he's done for, then it's no-body's —"

Danbo swore angrily to cut the bigger man short. "Didn't I tell you to keep hands off Speer?"

"Sure. But how the hell could we, him havin' the bag?"

"No matter," Danbo said grudgingly after a moment's thought. "If he was able to cut Clyde down, he's alive."

"Damn him for what he did to Clyde! I hope he cashed in."

"And I hope he didn't. Now you better get down and watch this."

Kelso stepped aground and stood alongside Danbo as the gambler went to one knee and, holding his slicker open, shielded a match he wiped alight across the buckle of his belt. By the match's flare Kelso watched him open the satchel and take a sheet of paper from it.

This, Kelso knew, was the bill of lading the bank always sent along with a gold shipment to Wells-Fargo. He leaned down now and peered at it, saying in disgust, "Only fourteen thou-sand."

"Not too good. But not too bad either. After last week they were playing it safe."

The match flared out, and as Danbo was reaching for another Kelso asked, "What hap-pens to Clyde's share?"

"It's yours, Matt."

"That's white of you, Lyle."

"Ever know me to short-change you when you did a job right?"

"Never did."

This gesture was typical of Danbo's long association with this man. He had Matt Kelso's loyalty for two reasons, one of which was his consistent generosity in dealing with underlings. The other was his knowledge of an incident in Kelso's past that, were he to go to the authorities with what he knew, would see the man hunted by every peace officer in this and adjoining Territories. Years back a U. S. Marshal had died mysteriously from a broken neck in a dark alley back in Bismarck.

"Let's see." Danbo had struck another match and spoke as casually as though he sat at the green-felted poker layout in his own home. "Your share's a quarter. Thirty-five hundred. Not bad for an evening's work."

"Not bad," Kelso agreed.

By the light of several more matches they divided the gold, the numbers on the several sturdy cloth bags and the listings opposite those numbers on the bill of lading making it an easy chore. Danbo even gave Kelso thirty-seven dollars more than was coming to him, preferring this to opening one of the bags and guessing how much should be taken from it.

The steady drizzle laid a whisper of sound through the trees as Kelso finally stepped over to stuff his share of the night's work into one of his saddle pouches. After he had buckled the pouch, he said, "Been thinkin' about what you said a while back, boss. About what happened to Clyde changin' things. I can't go back to the Point, can I?"

"No. Speer'll tie you in with Clyde after that ruckus yesterday. It'll take him about an hour of asking around town to know you weren't seen this afternoon."

"Then I've got to clear out?"

Danbo's answer was several moments in coming. "Don't think so, Matt. If you hole up on Rush's old homestead like you and Clyde did before I hired you on at the yard you'll be safe enough."

"Safe enough for what? I'm finished here."

"You're not, Matt. There's more in that bank safe, plenty more. They've got to ship it out. So I'll need your help again."

"But Rush's place is away the hell and gone off at the east end of that rim above town. How would I keep my belly filled loafin' day after day?"

"Easy enough. I'll be back home in two more hours. There'll be the usual game. It'll break up around two in the morning. Before I hit the bed I'll pack a sack of grub for you and leave it out in the wood shed behind the house. You can pick it up say along about three and be gone long before it gets light."

"Won't that black man of yours miss the grub?"

"Not if I tell him I took it to the crew in the

bunkhouse at the yard. I've done that before. He doesn't know I'm through at the yard."

Kelso had been rolling a smoke and now thumbed a match alight, staring at Danbo with a broad smile as he lit the cigarette. "It listens good, boss. Don't know what I'd do if I had to light out on my own."

"You won't have to light out. Just hang around the Rush place and sooner or later I'll turn up needing you."

Caroline Knight left the house shortly after ten o'clock the next morning and hurried down to the house corral where one of the crew had left her saddled bay tied to the gatepost. She at once swung astride the animal and headed out the lane to the main road, a mile distant.

The day was chill and bracing even with the sun shining intermittently through the thinning, broken clouds. The dampness brightened the brownish hue of the big meadow and the emerald of the pines beyond, and she took in the beauty of the day with a feeling of exhilaration so strong that she spurred the bay to a hard run once the track met the margin of the timber.

After letting the animal run the better part of half a mile, she put a curb on her strong impatience and drew him in to a crisp jog, shortly coming down on the town road. There she reined in to study the several wheel tracks plowed deep in the mud. All were broad, the marks of heavy wagons, and with that certainty she turned south up the road in the direction of Leesville.

The bay had carried her a good three miles before she briefly glimpsed the stage far ahead as it rounded one of the switchbacks low along the face of Lodgepole Grade. As she rode on to meet it, a hard excitement stirred in her until, abruptly becoming aware of it, she asked herself, *What is it about him?* And afterward she was puzzled and momentarily subdued in soberly considering the enigma of her emotions.

But that feeling soon died away. And when the stage presently drew even with her, its locked rear wheels making its tail end slew around in the drying mud, she looked up at Will Speer with a glad smile, saying, "The man with the hard head! Let's see that lump."

Will smiled ruefully, taking off his hat and cocking his head, drawling, "It's a beaut, Carry."

She caught her breath at sight of the swelling at the side of his head. "Now I know what Ned meant when he said Worts must have bent the barrel of his gun. Does it still hurt?"

At his shake of the head, she told him, "What happened to you was bad enough. If it had been anything worse I don't know what I . . . ."

She had said more than she intended, had shown him too much of her feelings. And now, embarrassed at having let her tongue slip, she looked away, glancing into the coach.

Her eyes widened in surprise then and she

said, "No passengers! How come?"

"The storm. Washouts all along the narrow gauge. They hadn't totted up all the damage when I pulled out. But the trestle over Sparrow Gulch is gone. So's the one off south below Baldy."

"No!" she breathed incredulously. "Then that means . . ."

"Means the line'll be closed for a month anyway, maybe longer."

"Why, that . . . That's awful, Will!" She sat a long moment considering the implications of what he had told her, then abruptly looked up at him to say, "Move over. I'll ride along with you."

"It'll cost you half fare."

"Try and collect it."

He reached down to take her arm as she stepped from the saddle to the wheel-hub then climbed up alongside him. He took her reins and stepped on back across the coach's roof to tie the bay's leathers to the rear luggage rail. Easing down on the seat alongside the girl then, he booted off the brake and lazily swung the whip to put the two teams in motion.

"I can hear Tom swearing already," Carry said. "This is serious, Will."

He shrugged. "The town can make out. The stores'll jack their prices and make a killin', of course. Food's been scarce before."

"I don't mean that. I'm thinking about the bank." She looked around at him, very aware of his bigness and solidness as her shoulder came against his with a sudden lurching of the coach. "The news Ned brought us last night was bad enough. Mainly because of you. But this makes things twice as bad. What's the bank going to do with the mines bringing more in every day?"

"The sheriff thought of that. He says he's willing to swear in enough deputies to keep a day and night guard on the place."

"But what happens when the month is up, when the trains start running again?" Carry took in his skeptical shake of the head, went on, "After last night it'd take a detail of cavalry to guarantee that gold getting safely to Leesville and aboard a train. Even then it won't be safe. They rob trains, you know."

Will was staring thoughtfully ahead, elbows on knees, the reins sagging in his hands. "There's got to be a way, Carry."

"Of getting the gold out? Now, with the trains not running?" She laughed, though there wasn't a trace of amusement in her voice. "Find one and they'll make you mayor, Will."

"A tempting proposition," he dryly stated.

He straightened then and snapped the leathers to send the teams on at a faster trot. "Did Ned make it before you folks had turned in last night?"

"Hardly. We don't often stay up till ten. It was later than that, come to think of it."

He gave her a frowning, puzzled glance, obviously surprised by what she had told him. But she didn't notice, and a moment later was saying, "Tom rode in this morning to see what Ned had found out about Kelso."

"Ten to one he's skipped the country. Or maybe my hunch was wrong and he had nothing to do with last night."

"What I can't understand is why Ned would hire men like Worts and Kelso."

"According to Ned he couldn't be too choosy about who he hired. Most men can make better wages at the diggin's than they can sweeping out stables and cleaning corrals. Or even driving a freight haul."

"According to Ned," the girl dryly echoed.

He looked sharply around at her. "Meaning what, Carry?"

"Meaning nothing in particular, I guess."

They rode on without speaking for an appreciable interval, until Carry all at once reached over and laid a hand on his arm. "That wasn't a kind thing to say, was it?"

When he only shrugged, she told him, "I could see it again in him last night, Will."

"See what?"

"What we were talking about yesterday morning. He was . . . Well, high-strung, nervous. Something's eating the boy."

"Something like having one of his stages robbed?"

His blunt sarcasm made her wince. "All right, I had that coming. Now that I've got this thing on my mind I always seem to be picking him apart, don't I? Yet —"

"You do," he cut in. "Which isn't like you. Why not quit thrashin' this thing around and give your mind a rest?"

"I'd like to, Will. Only last night after Ned had gone, Tom mentioned the same thing. He said he'd noticed it when you were all at the bank yesterday."

Will's every instinct was to keep strictly clear of any discussion of Ned's relations with Carry. Yet Tom Knight having found fault with his partner was something entirely different, and he drawled, "Go on, let's have it. What did Tom notice?"

"Only that Ned didn't seem to have his heart in it when the two of you were trying to change Baker's mind about sending the gold across."

"He didn't." Will smiled relievedly, thankful that her concern could be so easily explained away. "He shied away from the thing because of that stage they had stopped last week. Which he had a right to do, as it turned out. If I'd listened to him yesterday instead of arguing him into it, the bank wouldn't be out its fourteen thousand."

"You're wrong there," she came back at him. "They'd have waited another week or so, then tried it and maybe lost twice what they did."

They had reached an impasse, and there was an edge of real annoyance in Will's tone as he told her, "There's no straighter answer to any of this. Ned was right yesterday, I was wrong. In —"

"Then what would you do, call it quits? You

87

can keep on hauling feed and trade goods and such, sure. But do you leave the bank and the mines high and dry to haul the gold out themselves?"

"Not so long as I have any say in the matter."

"You've only got half the say, Will. Which is what I'm getting at. Ned's lost his nerve." She shook her head almost viciously, sighing her exasperation. "All I'm hoping for now is that the trip down the river on the *Belle* will smooth things over and let Ned get a hold on himself. Maybe if he can get away for a week or so he'll begin seeing things straighter."

When he made no comment, she eyed him speculatively for several moments, at length saying, "Why don't you come with us? On the *Belle*. It'd be like old times, the three of us together with nothing on our minds but enjoying ourselves. Tom could use an extra hand. He's taking a wagon load of truck down to the ranch and a fourth man would come in handy driving those horses back. You could . . . We could take the shotguns and do some bird hunting. Or if you're like you used to be, you could pack along one of Tom's rods and fish that swift water on the Humming Bird."

"And just who would run the yard while all this was going on?"

"Bailey would. With the trains not running you'll probably not make more than the three mail runs a week across to Leesville. Bailey can certainly handle those, along with the wagons

Belle settle herself more snugly on the mud that hadn't been here two days ago. Then, with a resigned shrug, he left the wheelhouse and took the ladder below.

Over the next hour he made several attempts to "grasshopper" the *Belle* off the mud by using the winches and the tall iron-shod spars that rose at the bow to a height almost matching the stern-wheeler's graceful twin stacks.

The spars, braced on the river bottom, were rigged with cables that lifted the boat's hull at the bow and allowed her to slide along the mud. Twice Hargutt felt the flat-bottomed hull inch forward. But after that nothing happened and the *Belle* remained where she was, as though glued to the bottom.

"Get a line ashore and we might winch her off," the mate suggested.

Hargutt shook his head. "Never been a winch made that would budge her as she is now."

For ten more minutes he paced the main deck, casting back and recalling all the tricks he knew. Not one of them would serve him now. Finally, completely disgusted, he headed for the ladder leading to the cabin deck.

He had lifted a boot to the first rung of the ladder when suddenly he halted. In another moment he wheeled around to bellow, "Horses, by God! We'll send to the Point for teams. Ten, twenty, a hundred if need be!"

So it was that the *Belle*'s skiff, with the mate at the oars, presently made for the south bank, sixty yards distant.

News of the *Belle* being aground up the river spread fast. By mid-afternoon, when Will and Ned drove their twelve teams down to the river bank some two hundred yards below the stranded stern-wheeler, they found a clutter of buggies and buckboards and saddle horses, and upward of fifty men and boys, gathered near the skiff where Fred Hargutt, the mate and several roustabouts waited.

Hargutt recognized Will at once, his expression brightening perceptibly as he walked over to him. "You be the one that had the beard. What happened to it?"

"Couple of my friends threatened to set the thing afire if I didn't cut it off," Will answered with a grin. He glanced in the direction of the *Belle* then asked, "Just what do we do here?"

Hargutt pointed in the direction of the skiff that rested with its bow on the bank close to a tall cottonwood. A heavy hawser tied about the tree sagged into the water on a line with the white packet. "We hauled that there two-inch ashore. Got it fastened to the heftiest mooring bit forward. You asked for a loggin' chain and block and tackle. We got them, too."

He turned to eye the teams, a displeased frown hardening the lines of his face. "Reckon that's enough horses?"

"Should be. Your man wasn't too sure about the block and tackle. Now that you've got one we'll try it first with six teams."

Hargutt's look was skeptical, though he said, "You're the boss from here on, so have at it."

Will was puzzled on one point, and now his glance shifted up the line of the river bank to a thicket of willows some five hundred yards distant that marked the mouth of Cat Creek. "If we make a straight haul on the line you've got laid out, won't we be pulling you onto deeper mud?"

"Thank the good Lord, no. That's what it looked like at first. But we made soundings from the skiff. Move me fifty feet toward that there tree and she'll be floatin' in seven feet of water."

With a nod, Will turned away. For the following ten minutes Hargutt closely watched as Ned and Will harnessed six of their teams to the heavy logging chain in the fashion of a jerk-line freight hitch. At length Will heaved a saddle to the back of the near animal of the rearmost team, by which time the roustabouts had chained one big pulley of the block and tackle to the cottonwood, threaded both pulleys with the hawser and secured the hawser's end to the tail of the logging chain.

A few moments later Will turned to Hargutt. "Want to stay here and watch or be on your boat?"

Hargutt swore good-naturedly, having completely forgotten this all-important detail. He turned away at once, calling back, "Give me two minutes after you see me aboard."

Ned came up to Will as, with a roustabout at the oars and Hargutt sitting the stern seat, the skiff pulled away from the bank and headed out into the swollen river. "What do we charge him for this, Will?"

"Just what I was wondering on the way out here." Will had been watching the skiff, but he looked around at his partner. "Why not make a swap with him? If we pull him off that mud he can give you and Carry and Tom a free ride down to Elkton."

"So he can," Ned agreed in some surprise. "Which reminds me. The mate said they're in a hurry to finish loading tomorrow so they can leave the day after. Means we've got only one more day to get ready."

"Then you'd better get the word to Tom and Carry."

"No chance of you changing your mind and coming with us?"

"Not any."

Those two clipped words of Will's somehow irritated Ned. He had been thoroughly ill at ease around Will today, ever since his friend had driven the stage into the yard with Carry sitting the driver's seat alongside him. To begin with, Ned's conscience had been bothering him over what had delayed him across in Leesville last night. Then, shortly after the stage arrived, another thing had nettled him.

He had never before been made quite so aware of how completely different Carry and Will seemed to be when in each other's presence. He had particularly noticed it in the office this morning when Carry had been teasing Will in trying to persuade him to make the trip down the river to Elkton. Carry had been in one of her gay, nimble-witted moods he had so seldom seen of late. And Will, ordinarily undemonstrative and sparse with his words, had unexpectedly responded in kind to the girl's lighthearted baiting.

Ned had been both surprised and puzzled at discovering this willingness in Will for matching wits with Carry. He supposed he had been a trifle jealous in not being able to join them in their byplay. Will's two-year absence had changed him, it seemed, had given the man the faculty of getting along with Carry in much the same straightforward give-and-take fashion as her father did. This stood in strange contrast to his memory of Will's former shyness and tongue-tied manner whenever he was around the girl.

He could remember a time when he had also had the knack of getting along with Carry in exactly this same way. But over the past few months all that had changed; they no longer understood each other as they once had, and he found himself deeply envying his partner.

Will just now prodded him from his indrawn mood. "By the way. Carry says it was after ten before you got to Crow Track last night. What held you up?"

"Just what the hell does it matter what did?"

Those angry words were spoken before Ned quite realized it, coming as an unconscious reaction to what he had been thinking. His friend's expression of amazement and bafflement roused a hard alarm in him, and he instantly sensed that his outburst had been uncalled for, a bad mistake.

"Now why am I combin' you over?" he was quick to say, smiling guiltily. "Couldn't be your fault that that nag of Worts went lame. Anyway, I could've walked it faster than he carried me."

Will studied him briefly in a frowning, disconcerting way, finally drawling, "Just wondered was all."

In another moment the mate was hailing them. "All set up there!" and Will turned away to pick up a bull whip lying on the ground near by.

He walked on over and stepped up into the saddle as Ned, relieved at the interruption, hurried up along the line of teams to take a stand between the leaders and reach for a hold on their bit-chains.

At the crack of the whip the teams lunged into motion, Ned moving quickly backward as the animals plodded forward, taking the slack out of the hawser. Shortly, with the block and tackle's pulleys creaking to the strain, the tightened hawser rose clear of the muddy water all the way out to the *Belle*'s blunt bow. Then slowly the teams drew to a halt, leaning against harness as the two big pulleys came together.

The mate used a wedge to lock the hawser in the rear pulley, and two minutes were spent with the roustabouts spreading the pulleys once more while the teams circled back and a new tie was made to the logging chain. Then the mate knocked the wedge loose, Will shouted and swung the whip and Ned steadied the heads of the lead team as they leaned into the harness once again.

Slowly, surely, the six teams strained ahead foot by foot. A ragged chorus of shouts came from the onlookers. Then suddenly the animals picked up the pace to a deliberate walk, Ned jumped out of the way and it was over, the *Belle* visibly drifting into the sluggish back eddy to shoreward of the mud bank.

A deck hand cast loose the hawser from the packet's blunt bow, her big paddle wheel began turning slowly in reverse, and she was definitely swinging toward the bank as Ned and Will set about unsnapping harness from the logging chain.

In five more minutes the *Belle* nudged the shore long enough to pick up the mate and the roustabouts with their gear. Hargutt leaned out of the wheelhouse and called through a speaking trumpet, "You with the horses, we'll settle up to-night in town."

Both Will and Ned waved an answer, then watched the packet drift out into the river again and slowly turn her bow in the direction of Rock Point. By the time they got the teams lined out and started away from the river bank, most of the crowd of watchers had driven or ridden away in the direction of the Bend road.

They had covered better than a mile when Ned, at the head of the line of horses, was startled at hearing a sudden whooping shout from Will at the rear. He glanced quickly around in time to see Will kick his horse and come toward him at a lope.

"Ned, we've got this thing licked!" Will's tone was exultant, almost a shout as he drew in alongside his partner. His eyes were bright with excitement and all at once he laughed lustily, saying, "We're going to get that gold of the bank's out of here! All in one chunk. And not a soul besides you and me and Tom and Baker will know we did it."

Ned, genuinely awed by his friend giving way to such a rare outburst, asked, "How do we do it?"

"On the *Belle*."

When Ned's glance showed nothing but strong puzzlement, Will went on urgently, "Don't you get it? No one'll dream of our moving the stuff till the trains are running again. This morning Carry mentioned Tom taking a wagon load of supplies down to the horse layout. So tomorrow night after the town's gone to bed, we load the gold on the wagon and drive the wagon down onto the boat. When we get to Elkton and the ranch, we swap for a lighter rig and take the gold across to Junction, put it aboard a train off east of where the line's washed out. It's that easy."

Ned, quick to grasp the possibilities of this startling idea, was nonetheless slow in sharing his partner's enthusiasm. The complication of his personal affairs had lately made him unnaturally wary, even suspicious of anything that might further complicate them. But as he considered Will's suggestion, he found himself abruptly reasoning that here might be one sure way of saving himself from any further involvement with Danbo. No sooner had the notion struck him than he was feeling a heady relief and a mounting excitement.

"Man, maybe you've hit on something!" He grinned broadly, delightedly. "We could do it! And if it works out, the whole sorry mess'll be cleared up."

"So it will, now that friend Kelso's skipped the country."

They talked about it all the way back to the Point, talked over each detail of loading the wagon tomorrow night and of getting it aboard the *Belle* without arousing anyone's curiosity.

Much later, with Ned gone for the day and the hands of the stage office clock nearing the hour of six, Will walked back along the lot to the barn corral to saddle an animal and leave for the homestead. A yard man was finishing up work at the corral and offered to rope a horse for him. He thanked him and watched him go into the corral.

His attention strayed as he took out his pipe, packed and lighted it. Only when the gate hinges squealed did he glance around to find the yard man leading a brown gelding from the enclosure. It was the animal they had found in the alley across in Leesville last night, the one Ned had ridden home.

"Can't use him," Will was quick to say. "He's gone lame."

"Lame? Him?" The man was obviously surprised as he looked around at the animal.

When his glance swung back to Will once more he shook his head. "You're thinkin' of some other jughead. This one's sound. I know because I forked him up to the diggin's and back not two hours ago. This here's a real prime piece of horseflesh."

Lyle Danbo had picked himself a place along the River House's long mahogany counter that let him look into the back-bar mirror and have a good view of the lobby through the wide doorway obliquely behind him. So it was that he saw Ned Oakes cross the lobby shortly after five-thirty and disappear in the direction of the main stairway.

He was deliberate in ordering another whisky and in downing it as he made small talk with the apron. Only after another five minutes did he lay a silver dollar on the counter, tell the man, "Buy yourself a buggy with the change, George," and then walk on out into the lobby.

To be seen visiting Ned's room had become such a commonplace thing that he wasn't caring who noticed him as he mounted the stairs, walked to the rear of the upper hallway and knocked on Ned's door.

On hearing Ned's muffled answer, "It's open," he pushed the door wide and entered the room to find Ned, face half lathered, standing in front of the bureau mirror with a straight-edge razor in hand.

Danbo schooled his expression to complete soberness as the other looked around. Ned, on the point of saying something, took in the gambler's impassive stare and waited until the door was shut before asking, "Why so gloomy, Lyle?"

Danbo deliberately took a stance to one side of the door, shoulders against the wall, his chill glance not wavering as he studied Ned. It was several seconds before he abruptly asked, "What did you do, offer him a bigger cut than I did?"

For an instant Ned's look was one of complete bafflement. The next, a high alarm flared in his eyes. "What're you trying to say?"

Very softly, Danbo breathed, "What was the deal you made Kelso?"

Ned's hand that held the razor began visibly trembling. His face lost color, became quite pale. "Kelso?" he echoed hollowly. "What makes you think I made a deal with him?"

"What makes me? This, my friend. I haven't seen Kelso since he and Worts left me back there in the alley and went to get the gold off that stage last night."

FOUR

Ned Oakes, facing Danbo there in his upstairs room at the River House, felt a stab of chill apprehension settle through him. He was struck dumb by what the gambler had just told him and he moved slowly over to the bed now to sit heavily on it.

It was several seconds before he found the voice to ask lifelessly, "What was that? Say it again, Lyle."

"Kelso got away with the gold off the stage in Leesville last night. How much did you pay him to give me the slip?"

The man's rough-edged words finally succeeded in rousing Ned from his stupor of incredulity. The color came back to his face and he burst out indignantly, "Me buy off Kelso? After all it meant to square things with you?"

He came up off the bed, brandishing the straight-edge. "Why would I want Kelso to cross you? With all I've got to lose."

Danbo eyed him coldly, aloofly. "That's what stumps me, why you'd do it. I could go to Caroline Knight and —"

"You do and I'll . . . I'll kill you, Lyle!"

Danbo, taking in the wild light in Ned's eyes, was hard aware of the razor that moment. This man could be very dangerous. He had been crowded too far. And with that sharp awareness the gambler's next words were spoken more mildly, "You mean he played us both for fools?"

Ned suddenly swung halfway around and with a vicious stab of the arm threw the straight-edge at the wall. Its blade bit deep into the wood, its ivory handle quivering. In a blind rage, he wheeled around to shout, "You lie! You got that satchel last night and —"

"Careful, Ned, careful!" For the space of perhaps three seconds Danbo stood with right arm rigid, ready to reach in under his coat to his shoulder holster. He was relieved then at seeing indecision and doubt gradually edge into the other's glance, and said quickly, "So that's it. He crossed up the both of us."

"You were there," Ned countered hotly. "Couldn't you see him and stop him?"

"I was with the horses. It was black as the inside of a barrel back in that alley. That shotgun cutting loose caught me by surprise. I waited as long as I thought I dared, then made tracks away from there in a hurry. He hadn't shown up by then."

"His jughead wasn't there when we found Clyde's."

"Then he just plain laid low and outsmarted me." Danbo sighed in pretended bafflement. "Probably watched me and pulled out right after I did. Which leaves us right back where we were, you and me."

"The hell it does! I passed the word to Kelso,

103

which was our bargain."

"Part of it, friend. Only part. We were to be quits when a halfway split took care of the five thousand you owe me."

Made speechless by helpless anger, Ned turned away and paced to the room's back window that looked out over the roof tops of Front Street below and on to the river. For a moment he stood staring sightlessly upon the scene as he tried to think of a way of beating down Danbo's cool logic. Then abruptly he was seeing the *Belle* moored at the levee and remembering what he and Will had planned for tomorrow night.

All at once a coolness threaded his nerves and he could think rationally once more. He was in complete control of himself when he turned around to say, "Lyle, there was fourteen thousand taken off that stage last night. Which would've canceled out the five I owed you. So I say we're quits on the thing."

"And I say we damn well aren't quits."

Danbo waited for Ned to argue this and, when he didn't, drawled, "Get this through your hard head. No man alive's ever gone back on a debt he owed me. Alive, I said. So think it over a few days and we'll talk about it when you can see things a bit straighter."

"A few days from now I'll be down in the Elkton country helping Tom bring that bunch of horses back. We'll be gone two weeks anyway."

"Doesn't matter. We've got plenty of time for this," Danbo blandly remarked. "No trains'll be running for the next month at least. Which means the bank couldn't clean out that vault if it had to."

Ned had nothing to say to this. And the gambler, reaching out to open the door, shed his severity and let his face relax into an apologetic smile. "No hard feelin's, I hope. I couldn't really believe you'd thrown in with Kelso. But I had to find out."

Ned's only reaction to this was a spare lifting of the shoulders, whereupon Danbo told him, "This is tough on the both of us. Forget what I said about you and Kelso. When you're back from Elkton we'll put our heads together and figure out something."

He turned then and left the room. And long after his steps had faded down the hallway Ned stood motionless, staring bleakly at the faded flowered paper on the wall opposite.

Presently he leaned down tiredly and pulled open the bottom drawer of the bureau, rummaging under some clothes until finally he lifted out a flat, stoneware whisky bottle. He uncorked it, put it to his mouth and tilted it, taking several swallows. He grimaced in distaste as he returned the cork to the bottle and put it back in the drawer.

His thoughts were a jumble as he lathered his face once more and finished shaving. He felt the blood mount to his head as he thought bitterly of Matt Kelso. He had naturally never trusted the man, yet neither had he given Kelso the credit for having either the wits or the courage even to try to trick Lyle Danbo. It was plain now that Kelso must have acted on the spur of the moment after seeing Clyde Worts fall at the blast of the shotgun. He must have known that Danbo couldn't see him in the pitch-blackness of the alley. The weight of the satchel had probably told him he was carrying what to him would be a small fortune. He had made his gamble against long odds and it had paid off handsomely.

For some moments Ned weighed the possibility of Danbo having deceived him completely, of Kelso having handed over the gold in spite of the gambler's claims. Yet as he thought back on his dealings with Danbo he ruled out the chance that the man had been lying, for he couldn't recall one instance when Danbo had been dishonest or anything but straightforward with him.

Hardly had he made his admission of Danbo's seeming honesty toward him than he was remembering how he had just now deceived the man in not telling him of his and Will's plans for the *Belle*. Danbo, stung by last night's failure, would logically expect him to pass along the word of any move the bank was making. He hadn't passed that word, didn't intend to, though now as he weighed the chances he was taking in tricking the gambler he knew that the man must never be given the slightest inkling of how the gold had been taken out.

Somehow he would have to impress upon

Will, upon Tom Knight and Baker — and eventually Carry, of course — that the mystery of how the bank had solved its knotty problem could never be explained even to close friends. Danbo, meanwhile, would remain in complete ignorance of what had happened. If he did manage to discover that the bank's vault had somehow been all but emptied, then he, Ned, would simply say that it had been done without his knowledge.

His reasoning in all this was complicated but nonetheless sound, he decided. His only obligation to Danbo was the settling of his debt, and now he further reasoned that more gold would be coming in from the mines while he was away on the Elkton trip. By the time he returned, and when the trains were running to Leesville again, Danbo would have another chance to make good last night's loss.

He closed his mind to looking that far ahead, to facing the fact that he would one day again have to betray Will by planning the robbing of one of their stages. It was enough to think of the matter at hand and to relish the much-needed sop to his conscience in knowing he hadn't betrayed Will or Tom or Carry tonight in his talk with Danbo.

By the time he left his room and went down into the lobby, headed for the dining room, this awareness of having remained loyal to Will tonight was crowding out his worry and depression. For the first time in a long time he could take pride in something he had done; he could almost, but not quite, risk looking himself squarely in the eye because of having done the right thing.

He ate his supper, sitting alone out of choice at one of the small corner tables. The waitress, on bringing him his plate, smiled down at him to say, "You look cheerful tonight, Mr. Oakes."

"No reason why I shouldn't be, Lily. Unless I find this meat's tough."

"You won't. I cut you a nice piece."

By the time he had finished the meal and was on his way out of the dining room his solitary mood had changed and he was feeling the need of someone's company. His first thought, after rejecting that of going into the bar and sitting in at one of the gambling layouts, was of riding out to the homestead to spend the evening with Will.

But the notion had no sooner struck him than he cast it aside, knowing that two minutes with Will would only put him on his guard again as he had been last night and all day today. Much as he longed to push aside the barriers that stood between his and Will's resuming their former easy-going relationship, he knew that time alone could ease the tensions now standing between them.

He could go on out to Crow Track, of course, and tell Tom of Will's idea about the *Belle* even though he and Will had earlier decided that Will was to ride out and see Tom first thing in the morning. Yet if he did pay the Knights a visit tonight he would have to be on his guard with them as much as with Will. For Carry had lately confounded him by her quietness and a certain odd way she had of seeming to be standing off and judging him for reasons known only to herself.

Several times he had been on the point of asking her point-blank why she had so subtly changed in manner toward him. But on each occasion he had hesitated, afraid of how penetrating her answer might be. He was hiding too many things to run the risk of bringing the question of their strained relationship into the open.

Finally, as he stood there in the lobby debating what he should do, his restlessness and loneliness drove him to choosing the course he had taken so many times of late. It wasn't yet seven o'clock. By nine he could be in Leesville. There, in Grace Drew's restful and stimulating company, he could forget his cares and think of nothing but the pleasant.

The fact that he so eagerly left the hotel and walked up to the stage yard to get a horse at the corral, without so much as a qualm over the choice he had made on how he was to spend the evening — or even a thought of Carry in relation to that choice — was symbolic of the change the past weeks had wrought in the man. He would have been outraged, horrified, had anyone suggested that he no longer knew the difference between right and wrong. He did know the difference, know it well. He would have argued that force of circumstance only made it seem that he didn't know the difference.

Yet one thing that he wasn't aware of — a thing he would have just as vehemently denied — was that somewhere along his back trail he had cast loose his integrity.

Will, supper finished, sat with his back propped against the trunk of the only tree within several hundred yards of the homestead cabin, a thinleaf cottonwood. As he drew on his pipe, idly scanning the thickening shadows off across the meadow, he was doggedly trying to unravel the enigma of Ned having lied to him about the brown gelding.

He had carefully inspected the animal's hoofs, finding no bruise, no telltale swelling, all the shoes tight. It was obvious that Ned had this afternoon been trying to hide something from him.

What that something might be confounded him completely. Ned wasn't the kind to brood over anything. The Ned he had known before leaving here two years ago would have come to him with any serious worry, regardless of his being in the right or the wrong. This new Ned wasn't the same.

Looking back across these three days since he had walked off the *Belle*'s gangplank, Will could recall half a dozen instances when Ned's manner had puzzled him by its furtiveness. The man's show of temper this afternoon was in itself proof of something being very wrong, or so it seemed.

Finally there was what Carry had said this morning, that both she and Tom had sensed a change in Ned.

Will's relations with his friends had always been straightforward, either black or white with no half-tones, no degrees of shading in his trusting or not trusting, liking or not liking man or woman. It was intolerable to him now to be undecided about Ned, the one man who had ever been really close to him.

It was this that presently sent him to the corral to throw a saddle on the brown gelding and head out along the town road. He was tying the gelding in front of the River House shortly before eight o'clock.

Ned wasn't in his room, the clerk in the lobby had seen him go out on the street something like an hour ago. So Will spent the better part of twenty minutes stopping in at the saloons along Grant Street. He was on his way back to the hotel when, on the off-chance of learning something, he turned into the stage yard and walked on back to the bunkhouse.

He found only one man, the blacksmith, in the crew quarters and remembered that his name was Howell. The blacksmith sat at the long room's single small table playing solitaire with a grimy deck of cards. As Will came in he looked around, arching his brows in faint surprise when he saw who it was.

"Ned been around tonight, Howell?" Will asked without preliminary.

The blacksmith nodded. "Came in, threw his hull on that white-stockinged mare and rode straight out."

"Any idea where I could find him?"

Howell's glance slid away too quickly as he answered, "None at all."

Will at once suspected that the man wasn't telling the truth. He also suspected that there was no reasonable way of making him tell what he knew, if in fact he knew anything.

Nonetheless he pretended disappointment and said ruefully, "Now wouldn't that be my luck? The one time I've needed to see him real bad since I got back."

The blacksmith's look showed concern. "Something gone wrong?"

Will shrugged. "Hope not. But it's either see him tonight about this or not at all."

Howell out of politeness wasn't going to ask point-blank what the trouble might be, which was something Will was counting on as he turned back to the door, grumbling, "Damn!"

He was stepping out through the doorway when Howell said, "Hold on a minute." He waited until Will swung to face him once more. Then, "You ain't going to say who told you this?"

"Told me what, Howell?"

"Where the boss went. Maybe where he went, I mean."

"No, I'm not going to say."

Howell smiled in a faintly apologetic way.

"Now I don't say I know this for sure. But if you got to see Oakes, you just might find him across in Leesville at the widow Drew's."

"Drew? A widow?" Will's puzzlement was patently honest.

"Yeah. Pretty young filly that tied up with Len Drew before he let the bottle get to him. You probably never knew him, but he's the one that set your barn afire across there and got burned to a crisp along with it."

Will remembered Carry's mention of Drew and Drew's widow now and nodded. "Yes, I heard about him. But what's Ned seeing his widow for?"

Once again that furtive quality edged into the blacksmith's glance. "As to that, I'm not the one to say. But he spends time with her, so the boys tell me."

Suddenly Will understood what the man was driving at, and he was glad for the weak lamplight that let him hide the shock it gave him and the hard surge of anger that rose in him.

Howell evidently didn't notice anything out of the way, for he went on, "Of course, he might've gone some place else, you understand."

"Sure." Only after Will had turned out the door once more, his thoughts reeling at the implications of what he had just learned, did he think to say, "Much obliged, Howell."

He walked out across the shadowed yard, his spurs laying a metallic rustling against the stillness, and stood by the street gate for all of five minutes, at first disbelieving what the black-smith had told him, then knowing he had to believe it.

By the time he started back down the street toward the lights of the hotel his anger had died away and he was feeling little beyond a tolerant wonder at Ned's foolishness. Or perhaps, he admitted, there was good reason for his friend's outwardly shabby treatment of Carry Knight. Other men had countless times let their affections stray even when their loyalty was due such beautiful and intriguing women as Carry.

This was strictly Ned's affair, no one else's. The man's infatuation might well wear itself out without Carry ever knowing of it. But meantime Will thought he had his answer to Ned's strange burst of anger this afternoon on the subject of his tardy arrival at Crow Track last night. Ned had probably spent some time with the Drew woman before leaving Leesville.

Crow Track's headquarters sprawled across a sixty-acre pocket in the pine timber at the head of a vast meadow of wild timothy a mile and a half removed from the Rock Point-Leesville road. Will brought the brown gelding along the track leading to the layout just short of eight o'clock the next morning.

His first glimpse of the clutter of outbuildings and corrals roused a sharp nostalgia in him. His years of working on Crow Track had made it seem more like home than any other place ever would or could, probably because it had been during that interval that he had grown into manhood.

He brought the gelding down the lane at a smart jog, lifting a hand to a pair of men working alongside a head-high stack of cordwood at the wood lot as he went by. Beyond the big hay barn the track climbed past the log bunkhouse to a low bench, at the far end of which lay the main house.

It made an imposing structure with its two-storied white porch running the length of all four sides. Tom Knight had originally brought his family here to live in what now served as the crew quarters. Some years later he had begun the main house and, taking pride in his work, had built it of rammed earth with walls three feet thick, following the practice of his Virginia forebears.

Will could clearly recall that the deep-set windows were fitted with heavy inside shutters slitted for the use of a rifle. He could also remember the kitchen's square-puncheon floor which had been laid two years before the random-width pine of the doweled flooring in the other downstairs and upstairs rooms.

A sudden frantic cackling in the chicken pen off east of the house took his attention now and he looked over there to see Carry, an ax in hand, holding a flopping, headless hen by the legs. A moment later she looked his way, saw him and tossed the dying chicken aside to wave him a greeting. He lifted a hand to her, checked the impulse to ride across there, and continued straight on to the house.

He found Tom Knight working on the ranch ledger in the office to the rear of the house's kitchen corner. Because he saw Carry coming toward the house carrying the hen, he unceremoniously announced his reasons for being here and quickly told Tom of his notion about the bank using the *Belle* as a way out of its difficulties, finishing by saying, "Here comes Carry. Don't know whether you want her to know about this or not."

Tom's glance narrowed, and in another moment he was shaking his bead. "No. She'd never give it away on purpose. But let's don't run the risk." He smiled broadly then, clenching a fist and striking the desk top a solid blow. "Will, you've pulled this thing out of the fire! We'll get by with it."

"Will Baker go along with the idea?"

"Why wouldn't he, especially when it's such a surefire thing?"

By the time Carry came into the room, Tom had put a rein on his excitement and was able to keep a straight face as the girl asked Will, "Since when can't you spare the time to say hello?"

"Hello," Will said, poker-faced.

"I mean . . . You could have ridden over to say it."

"I did. From the homestead. Here I am."

"You know what I'm talking about," she bridled. "You could have stopped by the chicken house."

"Too many lice."

She gave him a disgusted, angry look. But then her manner suddenly changed, her glance took on a smug, knowing quality as she eyed first her father, then Will. "Just what deviltry are you two cooking up?"

Will arched his brows in a look of offended innocence. "Deviltry? Us two? Nothing like it. Haven't laid eyes on the place since I got back, so I thought I'd just stop by and give it a gander. Anything wrong with that?"

"Nothing. Except that it's twelve miles out and twelve miles back. And you're supposed to be a busy man."

"Carry, where's your manners?" Tom Knight put in gruffly. "Must you always be the brat and horn in when you're not wanted? Suppose we were talking business?"

"So-o," she breathed gloatingly. "You are up to something."

Will, knowing her as well as he did, could see that they would somehow have to satisfy her curiosity. He thought he knew of a way and now told her, "Guess we are, Carry. I've come after the wagon we're taking to Elkton on the *Belle*."

"We?" she echoed, her eyes opening wider. "Then you're making the trip?"

He nodded. "Got to thinking about it last night. With the trains not running there's no real reason why I shouldn't. Then there's the horses to be thought of."

She was puzzled in seeing what he was getting at. "What horses?"

"The ones we're going down after. Ned isn't too sharp when it comes to having a wind-broke nag or two palmed off on him by as good a horse trader as Tom. So I thought to tag along and see we get our money's worth."

Carry suddenly reached over to her father's desk and snatched up a shot-filled leather paperweight. Will ducked as she threw it. Then the two of them burst out laughing. And Tom Knight, watching all this from his chair at the desk, chuckled softly and thought, *Why couldn't she have picked someone like Will?*

Presently the three of them left the house and walked down to the wagon shed below the bunkhouse. As they came in on it Tom Knight said, "We'll have a nice tidy load. Two men'll be wintering on the layout down there, so we'd best take along three or four crates of preserved stuff from the cold cellar. Then there's block salt, say two dozen cakes. Eight or ten spools of barb wire you'll have to pick up in town, Will, along with a keg of staples. And . . . Oh, yes, one of Billy Price's new hogback stoves with ten foot or so of chimney pipe. Can you think of anything else, Carry?"

"Flour, salt, side pork —"

"The men can buy all that down in Elkton for a sight cheaper than we can get it here."

Tom called one of the crew across from the

barn and the four of them pushed the wagon from the shed, the crewman then going across to the barn corral to harness a team.

While they waited, Tom told Carry, "We'll go in late this afternoon and spend the night at the hotel. Hargutt will want to be starting downriver at the crack of dawn."

Carry looked at Will. "Do we take along shotguns for a try at grouse?"

He nodded. "And you said something about a rod. If Tom doesn't object."

"Two rods," Tom put in. "One apiece for you and me. If I remember right, the last time we wet a line I beat the tar out of you."

This pleasant interlude was the kind Will had been hungering for off there on the reservation when he had so abruptly made up his mind to draw his pay and head for home. It struck him now that for the first time since he had set foot on the Rock Point levee he was completely at his ease with no immediate worry or doubt plaguing him, no need for being on his guard in what he said or did. Tom and Carry Knight were comfortable people to be around, cheerful people. They unconsciously put a man at his ease by being so natural and straightforward, this in striking contrast to Ned's changed manner that seemed invariably to put a man on edge without his quite knowing why.

He was going to enjoy the trip down the river, especially since he had last night found at least a partial answer to Ned's nervousness and short temper. From now on he could blithely ignore any of Ned's quirks that might otherwise cause friction, and he had the hope that Carry and Tom would do likewise if any unpleasantness came along.

Once the blacks were hitched to the wagon they drove on up behind the house to the root cellar and began loading. Carry insisted on packing the food crates, having her own ideas about what canned fruits and vegetables should be taken along. Finally, with the food loaded, they went into the kitchen and spent a quarter-hour over coffee, Tom asking question after question about the cavalry's campaign against the Nez Perces.

Will's hesitant, spare-worded answers gradually took on meaning to Carry, who presently asked him with typical bluntness, "Then if it was such a bungled up mess and such a waste of time, what took you so long to call it quits and come home?"

He could have answered her honestly by telling her that she had been the main reason for his staying away. Unable to do that, he answered somewhat lamely, "A man always kept hoping things'd change for the better. Maybe they have by now. Then there was the pay. It was good."

"Good!" Carry echoed dryly. "It was maybe a quarter of what you could have been taking out of the business if you'd been here."

Just then Will was thinking, *Now we're back at*

it again. He didn't want their talk to keep on in this vein and, trying to think of a way of stopping it, was saved the trouble by Torn, who had evidently noticed his discomfiture. "We're wastin' time sitting here gabbing, you two. Let's be at it."

So, after this briefly disquieting interval, Will found the rest of the morning to be just as pleasant as it had been. When they climbed into the wagon to drive on down to the storehouse, he was in hopes that Carry would remain at the house, for he wanted to talk to Tom about the details of loading the wagon at the bank tonight. But Carry tagged along to help them load the salt and the heavy spools of barb wire.

This last was hard work, and Will marveled at Tom Knight's ruggedness in staying with it. Tom's hair was graying, his face had thinned down over the years and taken on a hawkish, weathered look. But he was still a vigorous, tough-fibered man, and only when they had heaved the last spool of wire into the wagon bed did he lean against the end-gate and remove his hat to mop his brow, breathing heavily as he said, "Time was when I could've stayed with a job like this by the hour, breathin' easy. Now look at me."

"I've been looking." Will, also short of breath, glanced at Carry. "Can't you make him slow down?"

"Just try and make him. He's knuckle-headed and won't listen. So I gave up long ago."

The two men filled their pipes and stood there making idle talk, both hoping that Carry would lose interest and go on up to the house so that they could make plans for seeing Baker and for the night. But the girl didn't leave, in fact seemed to enjoy listening to them. So presently Will gave up and climbed into the wagon announcing, "Time to go."

They rode along with him to the house, where he got down to tie the gelding's reins to a rear side-brace of the wagon. It was after he had climbed back into the wagon that Tom managed to give him a meaningful look and tell him, "We'll be bringing a surrey in with our baggage and gear. How about leaving it at the yard while we're away?"

"Sure thing."

"Then I'll see you along about three. Have to make a stop at the bank to tell Baker about our trip before he quits for the day."

On the way out to the road Will idly wondered why Tom had decided that Carry shouldn't know what was being loaded into the wagon tonight. But then when he thought of what this could mean to the bank, and to Tom, he understood. Tom Knight wasn't taking any unnecessary chances, not one.

Once every now and then only one or two players — or sometimes no one at all — showed up at Danbo's house for the nightly game. Tonight was one of those times, Red Byrd, owner of the Oriole mine, being the only man on hand by nine-thirty.

Danbo, always willing to gamble, suggested blackjack. They played for the better part of an hour, the deal switching back and forth, Danbo winning consistently. Finally Byrd tossed the deck aside in disgust. "Not my night, Lyle. Let's call it quits."

Danbo nodded and reached over for the cigar box at the table's edge, offering the mine owner one of his fine Havanas. "How're you boys going to make out with your concentrates now that the trains aren't running?"

Byrd shrugged his powerful shoulders. "Going to rig a bin for mine and put a guard on it till we can haul again."

"And what'll the bank do with more of the pure stuff coming in every day?"

"Baker's talking about using guards, too. It's one hell of a note, Lyle."

"So it is."

Byrd rose to leave after several more minutes. And Danbo, at a loose end for spending the rest of the evening, decided to do what he had on several other such occasions. When they went into the hallway, he followed Byrd's example in reaching his hat and overcoat down off the mirrored stand by the front door, saying, "Think I'll walk along with you as far as the War Paint. Might find a good game going."

"Not for me, not tonight."

They parted company halfway down along

Grant Street at the hotel, where Red Byrd had a room. Danbo, feeling the night's chill, quickened his stride and presently swung off the walk and through the doors of the War Paint, finding the saloon only moderately crowded on this weekday evening.

He found Charley Forrest, the owner, sitting the lookout's stool at one of the faro layouts and asked him, "Where's the big game tonight, Charley?"

"Back table," Forrest answered agreeably, for it was their habit to pass business back and forth between them, Danbo drawing the players with a taste for really high stakes, Forrest the ones who found they couldn't afford Danbo's game.

Danbo made a fifth at the back table. He knew three of the players and spoke to them by name before taking one of the empty chairs. And as he began playing he followed his usual practice when gambling here of never betting too extravagantly and of now and then folding a possible winning hand just for appearances' sake. His method of play had paid off, he knew, for even as a professional gambler he was invariably welcomed into a game by men who knew him.

After the first hour he was thirty dollars the winner. After the second his winnings had been whittled down to little more than twenty dollars. By midnight he was four dollars the loser and, not particularly interested in the game decided to call it a night.

Charley Forrest bought him a drink on his way

out, receiving in return one of Danbo's mild Havanas. Danbo started up the street feeling that the evening hadn't entirely been wasted. For one of the men at his table, a stranger, had been reckless with his money even though losing and had shown more than a passing interest when one of the others mentioned the nightly high-stake game up at Danbo's house on Lupin Street. The gambler suspected he would see the man again, and in his own parlor.

He presently came to the long, deserted stretch of walk leading past the stores on upper Grant above the hotel. Just why he happened to glance across the way at the darkened, barred window of the bank he was never to know. But he did look that way.

His glance was swinging ahead once more when, out of the corner of his eye, he caught a faint glow of light reflected in the bank's window. His eye shuttled back there again in time to see the light more plainly. Then in two more seconds it flickered out and was gone to leave the window in total darkness once more.

Pausing at the walk's edge, Danbo wondered if his imagination might be working overtime. But then, sure he had seen a light, a faint excitement began to lift in him. Someone was either now in the bank, or had been only seconds ago.

He was standing there trying to decide what to do, go across the street and look in the window or go down to the hotel to try and find the night marshal, when all at once a jingle of harness chains and the heavy rumble of a wagon echoed hollowly from somewhere behind the buildings across the way. That sound held on, and Danbo, now thoroughly curious, moved warily back across the walk to take a stand in the pitch-black well of a store's inset entrance.

So it was that he shortly saw a team and wagon draw out of a narrow side alley two doors above the bank. The team swung toward him at a slow jog and in a few more seconds the wagon was rattling past him, bringing him more stiffly erect as he made out two figures sitting the seat.

One was Ned Oakes. And the other man, unmistakable because of his size, had to be Will Speer.

Danbo, bewildered by the sight of this pair abroad at this time of night, was completely confounded when he added their being here to what he had seen a scant minute ago, the light flickering in the bank's window.

Now, watching the wagon pull away in the darkness, he became further mystified on seeing it swing sharply to the right and disappear into the head of a steep-pitched and narrow side lane he knew led down to Front Street and the river.

He was almost positive that Ned and Speer had been inside the bank. *Why?* he asked himself, and felt a tingling run along his spine as he could think of but one obvious answer to his question.

That moment a muted, metallic rattle sounded across to him from directly opposite.

His glance had no sooner swung to the front of the bank once more than he was seeing a figure faintly outlined in the darkness against the building's doorway. Then in another moment that figure moved down the walk toward the lights of the hotel and the saloons at the center of town.

Abruptly whoever it was across there left the walk and cut obliquely toward this side of the street. Danbo moved out of the doorway, watching as the man's shape moved between him and the lights further down the street. He caught his breath sharply as recognition came.

This man was Tom Knight.

Danbo stood in a paralysis of incredulity, trying to make sense of what he had just seen. Why should Ned and Speer, along with Tom Knight, be paying this furtive midnight-hour visit to the bank? Why should they be using a wagon? And why had they left the place separately?

Suddenly Danbo had a thought that came with the force of a sledge-hammer blow between the eyes. He could feel his pulse pounding at his temples as excitement hit him. And almost without thinking he moved out into the street and then across it, ignoring the far walk so that his steps would be muffled as he hurried to the head of the alleyway down which the wagon had turned.

When he reached it the first thing that caught his eye was the neatly spaced row of coal oil lanterns marking the line of the *Belle*'s main deck beyond the levee below. Then in another moment he made out the wagon and team pulling in alongside the foot of the river steamer's staging plank.

Danbo stood there for a good quarter-hour, until he was sure. Several times he glimpsed shadowy figures moving up and down the *Belle*'s gangplank, and presently he saw the wagon's team being led away by someone he thought might be Ned. Throughout this interval his excitement remained at a high pitch as he gradually became more positive of the meaning of what he was seeing.

Finally he witnessed something that was all the proof he needed of a growing conviction. Eight or ten men, two of them carrying lanterns, filed down the gangplank onto the levee and gathered about the wagon. Then in several more moments he watched them turn the wagon and slowly push it up the stage onto the *Belle*'s foredeck, the biggest man among them — and he was certain that this was Will Speer — holding the wagon's tongue clear of the planks.

The lanterns down there presently moved off the foredeck to leave it in semi-darkness. He kept an eye on the gangplank for several more minutes and didn't see a man cross it to the levee. Finally he turned away and walked quickly up the street in the direction of his house, his thoughts weighing the things he had to do throughout the remaining hours of the night.

First of all he would have to get out to Rush's

abandoned cabin and find Kelso. That was no more than an hour's ride each way. When he got back to the house he would have to pack a small trunk and probably a suitcase. Finally, he would have to make sure of getting his belongings down to the levee early, very early in the morning.

Danbo didn't yet know how he was going to explain his presence aboard the *Belle* when she started downriver in the morning. But he would think of a likely story, a good enough one to give him the chance of proving his hunch on what he thought had been loaded aboard the wagon in the alley behind the bank tonight.

FIVE

The *Belle* and the levee lay in the chill shadow of the high eastern rim, but early morning's strong sunlight played brightly across the still swollen river and the far shore as Carry and Ned, wearing coats and standing at the forward rail of the cabin deck, watched the roustabouts below moving in and out along the broad staging plank, loading the last of a clutter of barrels and crates from the levee onto the main deck.

Ned had surprised and pleased Carry by his cheerfulness ever since joining her and Tom Knight in the hotel dining room for an early breakfast. He had several times laughed in the hearty, near-boisterous way she had almost forgotten. And as he had been driving them down here in a buckboard he had once surprised her by impulsively putting an arm about her waist and looking past her to say to her father, "Tom, what say we stretch this thing out and take an extra week gettin' back? I'm sick of the sight of this town. Do us all good to loaf and be away a while."

"Suits me." Tom, a trifle startled by this unexpected pronouncement, had added, "But let's see how we feel a week from now. If I know Will he'll be itching to get back to work."

"Will was away for two years without itchin' to

130

get back." Ned's tone had been larded with a heavy irony. "So this once he can do what someone else wants for a change."

Now, standing close beside him and leaning with elbows braced on the rail, Carry was recalling his sharp-edged words as she peered idly below watching her father and Will, who were sitting on the tongue of Crow Track's tarp covered wagon just forward of the head of the staging plank. She hadn't until this morning known that Ned bore Will any animosity for his long absence. Curious as to why he should feel this way, she nonetheless decided to postpone asking him about it, not wanting to risk dampening his rare good spirits.

She looked around at him to catch his eye and nod below now. "You'd think those two would get up here and be more sociable. Or are they afraid someone's going to help themselves to what's in the wagon?"

Something she had said made Ned's glance move nervously away, made him smile and say quickly, "You never can tell about the gangs on these boats. Besides, girl, we don't need company. It's been a long time since we've been by ourselves, you and me."

"Too long, Ned." She reached over to lay a hand on his. "So beginning now, let's try and make up for it, shall we?"

Her fervent wish in that moment was to bring to life again that old feeling of closeness and trust she had once shared with this man. She supposed she had loved him back then; she knew she could still care for him in the same way if he would only crawl out of the shell he had so strangely used of late to hide his emotions.

Yet, as had happened so many other times, he didn't respond. Even as she spoke she noticed his glance straying toward the levee. He abruptly stiffened at something he saw down there, his face lost its ruddy tan and he breathed softly in awe, "I'll be damned! Where does he think he's going?"

She looked down there to see a handsome black pulling a buggy toward the foot of the staging plank, and recognized Lyle Danbo as the man holding the reins. His black man sat beside him with a wicker suitcase across his lap. A small brass-bound trunk rode in the rig's bed behind the seat.

"He must be coming with us, Ned."

Her curiosity had been roused by Ned's strange reaction at sight of the gambler. And now she grew even more curious at noticing the hard set of his jaw as he curtly nodded.

"You don't like the man?"

"Sure. Why wouldn't I?"

Ned's tone lacked conviction and it was plain to Carry that he had been caught off guard by her question. Baffled and irked by his volatile mood, she picked this moment to mention something that had been troubling her these past few days. "Ned, you never told us you were making him your partner. Tom and I didn't know till we saw the new sign on the yard gate the other morning."

He looked around at her with a slight flush tingling his slender face. "Didn't know myself until a day or two before the sign was painted. He'd been a big help, Carry."

"We didn't know about that either."

He smiled sparely, guiltily. "My fault. But for just that once I'd decided to try and go it alone. Danbo had offered to throw five thousand dollars into the business for a half interest. At first I told him I wouldn't need it. Then finally . . . Well, one thing after another piled up on me and it began to look bad. So in the end I made the deal with him. Guess I should've let you and Tom know about it."

"No, not necessarily." Carry sighed gently in regret over having let their talk take such a serious turn. "Besides, none of it matters now that Will's back and Danbo's out of it."

Ned seemed to be only half listening as he watched Danbo step down from the buggy and hail one of the deck gang to come for his trunk. Then from above came the sudden moan of the whistle to send several of the roustabouts running out along the levee to unhitch the *Belle* from the pilings.

Carry and Ned stood silently watching as Danbo and the last of the deck crew came aboard. Then shortly a capstan began rumbling, the heavy stage was drawn in and the *Belle* drifted out from the levee.

It struck Carry just then that Ned's solemnity was too contagious to be tolerated any longer, for from the outset she had eagerly and happily looked forward to the moment when the *Belle* should start downriver. So now she stepped back from the rail to say with forced heartiness, "Let's get down and see what Tom and Will are up to."

Ned wasn't even looking at her. He had faced around and was watching Lyle Danbo climb to the head of the wide railinged stairway some twenty feet away. "You go along, Carry," he told her, still eyeing the gambler. "I'll be down later."

She left him then, walking to the stairway. Danbo nodded to her, tipping his hat with a flourish as she passed. "Good morning, Miss Knight. A fine day to be on the river."

"A fine day, Mr. Danbo."

She had one last glimpse of Ned as she started down the stairs. His face seemed stiff, tight-set in anger as Danbo joined him. And Carry, completely mystified by what the past five minutes had shown her, hurried down the steps feeling a sense of release and a sudden strange longing to be with Will Speer.

Lyle Danbo was the soul of affability as he came up to Ned and held out his hand. "Wasn't sure but what you folks had changed your minds about going. Now that you haven't, it means at least the first part of the trip'll be bearable."

Ned ignored the gambler's hand. "How did you find out, Lyle?"

"Find out?" Danbo echoed in bland innocence. "Find out what?"

"You know damn well what! Who told you? How'd you know?"

The gambler let his jaw sag open in pretended bafflement. "Man, what're you talking about? How do I know what? All I do know is that I'm going down the river as far as Bismarck to catch a train to Omaha."

Ned shook his head savagely, for the moment speechless as he glared down at the smaller man. He knew he had said more than he intended, but his heady anger and his rock-solid conviction that Danbo must know what had been loaded aboard the wagon last night made him cast aside all caution.

Danbo, cocking his head in speculation, said gently, quietly, "Come to think of it you must be talking about last night. About you and Speer being at the bank with Knight and then bringing that wagon down here. Matter of fact, I just happened to be coming home after a late game at Charley Forrest's and saw you. It struck me as a deuced queer time for you two to be driving around the town."

"So you do know." Ned's tone was lifeless, utterly weary. "Suppose we lay off the small talk and get to the point. You're not —"

"Suppose we do," the gambler cut in. "Beginning with why you didn't count me in on this."

"Lyle, you try and lay a hand on that gold and I'll —"

135

"Whoa now, my boy! Just step off and take a look, see where you stand. I'd hate to have to say a thing or two to the right people."

"But good Lord, think what you'll be doing to me!" Ned's hushed tone took on a pleading note. "If anything happens, anything at all, Will and Tom'll know who's responsible. I've got —"

"Why would they? With the gang of rough-necks that's working this boat anything could happen to that wagon and what's in it. If it happens when you're standing watch over it, then it just happens, is all." Pausing, Danbo eyed Ned closely to ask, "You're taking turns standing watch, aren't you?"

Hesitantly, Ned nodded. "We are. Will stayed with it last night."

"Which means your turn'll come along tonight. Fine."

"Look, Lyle. I swear I'll rig it so you'll have your chance at an express box when we get back. But don't touch this. Tom and the bank couldn't last it out. The bank'd have to close its doors. Tom could even lose Crow Track."

"Wait'll I reach for my handkerchief and have a good cry," Danbo drawled caustically. He smiled coolly then, continuing, "I took one licking a couple nights ago. This time I don't take another. We'll split even. But we get what's in that wagon and if anything goes wrong it's your hide they'll be tearin' strips off of."

Ned reached up to push his hat back and wipe the beady perspiration from his forehead. The gambler, taking in his sickly look, remarked mildly, "Who's ever going to know about us if we play it right? I'll tie a gag in your mouth and maybe you'll have to take a lump on your head. Except for that neither of us'll have a thing to worry about. Now why not forget Knight and his bank and get our heads together on this?"

Ned turned away, thrust hands in pockets and paced across to the rail of the stair well, then back again. He seemed to have a better hold on his emotions as he faced Danbo once more to ask, "How will you manage your end of it? The minute you turn up missing they'll know who did it."

"Don't you worry about that. I won't turn up missing."

Ned's eyes went narrow-lidded. "Which means someone'll be helping you. Someone already on the boat or someone on the shore. Who?"

"Let's forget you asked that, friend. If you don't know you can't give it away. Besides —"

"Kelso?" Ned interrupted, his tone sharp, accusing.

"That's a poor question to be asking," the gambler coolly replied. "You know as well as I that Matt Kelso's at least a hundred miles from here right now and still riding."

"I don't know it."

"Don't you trust me?"

"No."

Danbo's lips drew out to a thin, hard line. His

glance didn't waver as it met Ned's boldly. "All right, so you don't. But, brother, you play along with me or —"

"That works two ways, Lyle. I can talk, too, tell what I know. Then where would you be?"

"You talk?" Danbo laughed softly. "Where's your proof of anything I've done? Just where? You don't have any, not any. And where's mine against you? First, there's Grace Drew. We can stop right there."

For a moment Ned had thought he'd dented Danbo's confidence. Now he saw he hadn't. The man was without nerves. Somehow, either through calculation or just plain luck, he had managed to accomplish what he had just claimed; he had left Ned without a shred of proof against him throughout their several excursions beyond the limits of the law. And apparently he had planned this bold move just as sagely as he had the others.

Bleakly, resignedly, Ned accepted the fact that he was pitting his wits against a better, a shrewder, man. He stood a long moment trying to foresee the consequences of his giving in to the gambler. Then, as had happened so many times before, he closed his mind to what those consequences might be and said wearily, "Tonight then. Late, after midnight. Will tells me they tie up along the bank right after sundown. Which ought to be a help to you." As an afterthought, he bridled, "Only stay away from me from now on."

"And have Knight and Speer wonder what's wrong?" Danbo shook his head. "Nope, that'd never do. Matter of fact, by afternoon we may have a game going in the saloon. You might do worse than to sit in and make things look friendly like they're supposed to be."

Caroline had no sooner joined her father and Will at the wagon than she sensed that the main deck was strictly a man's world, no place for a woman.

Nonetheless she enjoyed being down here. She was quite aware of the bold stares of the roustabouts as they lugged part of the freight they had loaded this morning across to the hatches. Their language was as jovially coarse as that of range-bred men, but with a slight difference. Most men she had known always made it a point to speak mildly and politely when around a lady, whereas these roughnecks didn't seem to mind her overhearing their saltier offerings.

She blithely ignored all this in her fascination with watching what was going on along the crowded deck. Upward of a dozen men and boys were loafing near by, these being deck passengers who had paid next to nothing for their passage and had brought along their own provisions. They would sleep wherever they could find a place among the boxes, barrels, bales and sacks that crowded the fore part of the deck.

Carry had all but forgotten what it was like to

be aboard a river boat, though now memories of that other trip up the river four years ago when her mother was alive came flooding back to her. There were the same sounds and smells, the rhythmic pulsing of the engines, the sweetish odor of blended lubricating oil and live steam, the ring of the signal bell, the waterfall swishing of the big paddle wheel astern.

Stokers, bare to the waist, hauled cordwood to the boilers. A gangling boy was feeding the dozen or so horses — Crow Track's and Ned's and Will's among them — in a row of stalls running beneath the main staircase. Two deck hands were coiling lines near the capstans and at the base of the high "grasshopper" booms that might later be used to hoist the *Belle* over shallows and mud banks. There was an orderly confusion about all this that both intrigued and baffled her, making her begin to understand why Tom and Will preferred being down here for the time being rather than up above.

The three of them had been making only sparse conversation as they watched all this, and now Will caught her eye to ask, "Anyone else like to go up top for a look around?"

Carry realized that he was perhaps thinking she was embarrassed by what she was seeing and hearing down here. She was on the point of telling him how much she was enjoying it when, abruptly changing her mind, she answered, "I would." She looked at her father. "How about you, Tom?"

Knight shook his head. "Rather just stand here and soak in the sun while I watch someone else work for a change. You two go along."

She didn't, of course, realize that Tom had a very good reason for remaining with the wagon as she led the way across to the main stairway, where Will joined her. As they reached the head of the stairs she looked around to see Ned and Danbo still standing by the rail, their backs turned. That sight gave her an uneasy moment that passed quickly as she went through the wide doorway into the lounge, Will beside her.

Fred Hargutt had contracted for the building of the *Belle* in a Cincinnati yard seven years ago, his primary idea being that the packet's structure and accommodations should be suited to the navigation of the upper Missouri. Her saloon — running almost the entire length of the main deck — was as practically laid out as was her tough, shallow-draft hull. The long, high-ceilinged lounge boasted none of the gaudy splendor one found in the Ohio and Mississippi river boats, Hargutt's only concession to richness having been in paneling the big room with mahogany. In contrast, the rows of cabins flanking both sides of the room were walled with birch. All but a few stern ones, those reserved for the varied assortment of female passengers, were small and cramped, rigged with pairs of plain double-deck bunks.

Hargutt, as an economy measure, hadn't even bothered with the formality of installing the usual folding partition that at nighttime separated the men's and women's quarters on other boats, it being his bachelor theory that most women who traveled in the West weren't so overburdened with modesty but what they could pass between their cabins and the sanitary facilities in plain sight without undue embarrassment.

Members of families, men and women and children together, often shared these more desirable stern cabins. Tom and Carry had earlier been offered one of these and Tom had taken it once he made certain there was a draw curtain to pull between the two beds.

The *Belle*'s passenger list was a short one this trip, and as Carry and Will made their way down the saloon's carpeted center aisle there were less than a dozen men, and only three women, seated along the double rank of round oilcloth-covered tables, enjoying either coffee or whisky served by two colored waiters.

"Want to see our room, Will? It's next to the big one we had four years ago."

Carry led the way across to a door numbered *14* and pushed it open. The cabin was light and clean, plainly furnished with two wooden beds, a washstand and a single straight-backed chair.

Will smiled sparely as he looked in at it. "You're in luck. Ned and I drew one you couldn't whip a cat in. So I'll sleep on deck like I did last week. More air."

"And maybe fewer bugs?"

She laughed softly at Will's wry grimace, thinking just then how much freer and more at ease she felt in being around this tall man than she had some minutes ago in Ned's company. It wasn't a very charitable thought, she realized, though it was nonetheless a fact she had to face.

As they left the saloon by way of its rear door Carry asked, "All the way up?"

"All the way."

So they walked on back to climb the rear stairway — hardly more than a steep, railed ladder — to the hurricane. Up here, a good twenty feet above the river and with no railing to lend a feeling of safety, Carry quickly took Will's arm and pulled him in from the deck's edge.

The *Belle*'s superstructure was like everything else about her, practical in the extreme. The wheelhouse, lacking any ornamentation, stood on a waist-high platform so that its rear window could look out over the roof of the Texas, a double-cabin structure that provided living quarters for Hargutt, his mate and the occasional pilot Hargutt was compelled to hire between Omaha and St. Louis.

Hargutt noticed Will and Carry standing there and beckoned them across. "Help yourselves to that bench up for'ard," he told them, leaning out of the wheelhouse's window and pointing to a slatted bench sitting well ahead of the two towering stacks. "Best seat on the boat."

Will nodded his thanks and was turning away, Carry still holding his arm, when the captain called, "By the way, Speer. How would you feel about some meat huntin' come another hour or so?"

"Meat hunting?" Will didn't understand.

"Yeah. We swing a twenty-mile loop around some swamps and cattail brakes once we've taken on wood at Crampton's yard. Every time I run that stretch I spot maybe a hundred or two deer. Elk sometimes, too. Now if you hanker for the taste of a venison roast like I do, I can set you and your horse on the bank with a rifle. You can ride across that neck of land and meet us on the far side. It's only three, four miles, and if you have any luck at all you could snag us a couple of fat hindquarters for tomorrow night's supper."

Before Will could say anything Carry put in eagerly, "Will, would you . . . Could I go along? Or would I be in the way?"

"In the way? No." Will looked up at Hargutt then to ask, "Suppose we make slow time and you run off and leave us?"

Carry wasn't watching as the captain smiled meaningfully and closed one eye to Will, though she did hear him answer, "Not a chance of being left. Once you're on the far side you'll sight a big cottonwood standing all by itself over the brush. It's the only big tree around. If you're not there by the time we are I'll tie to the bank, have the crew bait some lines and catch us some bullheads. Best eatin' I know anything about."

Will eyed Carry questioningly, and she at once said, "I'd like to, Will. Say the word and I'll go

144

down right now and change."

"Then go ahead. And see if Ned or Tom would like to come along."

She left him to cross to the head of the ladder leading below. And as she disappeared Fred Hargutt observed in strict seriousness, "Once about every ten years or so I set eyes on something special like that and kick myself for bein' single. Speer, you got all the luck."

"Don't I wish I did have."

Will had spoken involuntarily, wanting to hide his embarrassment. What he had said startled him. But then, thinking about it, he knew he had spoken the truth.

For something like twenty minutes after Carry and Will had led their horses across the staging plank to the river bank they could see the *Belle*'s filmy banner of blue woodsmoke drawing farther into the distance to the north. Finally it disappeared altogether, and still they held their animals in to a walk, in no hurry at all to make time. For, as Will had observed after they came upon a bunch of four doe and a single buck less than three minutes after leaving the river, "If they're as thick as this, let's wait till we're on the far side and save ourselves packing the meat all that way."

So they continued on at a lazy pace, speaking only now and then, thoroughly enjoying the morning and each other's company. Tom hadn't been even slightly interested in joining them on the hunt. She had found Ned still talking to Danbo. He had been highly annoyed, she suspected, at the notion of her riding out alone with Will, though he hadn't said as much because of the gambler being there. And Carry, harking back to his strange behavior earlier, hadn't much cared what he thought of her going.

Thinking of that now, Carry wondered if her imagination was running riot this morning. But in recalling Ned's reaction to the sight of Danbo driving the buggy down the levee, she knew she was at least part way right in thinking that something unpleasant lay between the two men. What that something might be she couldn't even begin to guess, yet she couldn't see it as an excuse for Ned having spoiled one of the most pleasant moments she had enjoyed with him in weeks and weeks.

His edgy, unstable moods stood in sharp contrast to Will Speer's today or any other day. She doubted that Will under any circumstance would ever want to hide his feelings and shut himself away from her the way Ned had of late. Will, she judged, was incapable of any deviousness. He could be troubled or angry or hurt, the same as any man, but deceit was beyond him.

Being with Will this morning somehow reminded her of another time, eight or nine years ago when she was in her middle teens, when she had ridden with Will and her father on another hunt, one to track down a calf-killing grizzly. This day didn't in any way resemble that other one, for then it had been late fall and bitterly cold with a sifting of snow blowing. But she could clearly recall how satisfying it had been to be with Will, as it was now.

Though she had never admitted it even to herself, she supposed she had in a way worshiped Will Speer back then. He could handle a horse as well as any man she had ever known, gently or powerfully as the need arose. He had always been a fine shot, and good at reading sign. The only thing that had ever really irritated her about him had been his being so quiet, almost to the point of shyness. This had perhaps been one reason for her having gradually come to prefer Ned, whose outgiving and at times boisterous nature seemed better suited to her high spirits. Yet even after she came to see so much more of Ned, she had been very aware of a certain subtle something in the tall man's makeup that invariably stirred her more powerfully than Ned ever managed to rouse her.

She was thinking of this, wondering why it should be that Will still held that same sway over her emotions, when he abruptly announced, "There's our river. So we'd better get busy."

They had topped a low, brushy rise. Looking ahead she saw the line of the river something like a mile distant. The *Belle* wasn't in sight yet, nor was there any smoke showing along the northern horizon.

Will lifted a hand to indicate a higher hill close to the south. "I'll take a swing around that knob.

Looks like buckbrush along the far side. Might kick something out of it."

He drew the Winchester from its scabbard and laid it across the saddle's swell, and she said, "Will, let's take a buck and not a doe."

He nodded. "A youngster, not one with a big rack. And if we have luck we'll bring in all the meat. Never could see cutting off only the hind-quarters and wasting the rest."

He swung away from her, shortly calling back, "Meet you on the far side." And from then on his eye began probing each clump of brush and each dip in the ground, for this was ideal deer cover. He rode a hundred yards, another hundred, and saw nothing moving in the brush. Then presently he swung to his left behind the hill and, looking back, could no longer see Carry.

Off to his right lay a shallow dry wash. Until now he hadn't bothered to look beyond it. Once he did he saw the line of a weed-grown wagon track winding away to the southeast and idly wondered where it could lead. Presently he came to a sparse stand of stunted thinleaf cottonwoods and drew rein, bringing his horse to a stand as he sat listening, watching.

He had been sitting there motionless for perhaps thirty seconds when, from obliquely behind him, he caught the muffled hoof-falls of some animal. He looked quickly around and through the trees to see a rider leading a packhorse along the wagon track.

His first impulse was to ride on through the

trees and speak to this man, whoever he might be. But then it struck him that this would be pointless, for he had no desire whatsoever to pass the time of day with a complete stranger and perhaps spend so much time talking that Carry might begin to wonder what had happened to him. He was almost hidden, he doubted he could be seen, so he stayed where he was, leaning forward slightly in the saddle so that he could reach his horse's nose and cut off a whicker if the animal threatened to signal the stranger's.

The rider was soon out of sight beyond the trees. Will heard him draw on past, then presently saw him again, this time much closer than he had been.

Suddenly something about the look of the stranger's horse, a bay with one white front stocking, roused his curiosity. He had the feeling he'd seen the animal before. Yet the thought had no sooner struck him than he was questioning it, though he realized that this man might well have been in Rock Point within the past several days.

At any rate the matter wasn't important and he presently dismissed it from mind, by which time the rider and packhorse had dipped over a far rise and disappeared. He waited out another three or four minutes, not wanting to run the risk of a shot possibly attracting the stranger's attention. Then he rode out from the trees and along the side of the hill.

He didn't sight a deer for all of another five minutes. When he did he had already spotted Carry off to his left at a distance of perhaps a quarter of a mile. Four deer broke from a thicket of scrub-oak and bounded away to the north, almost on a line with Carry. He brought his rifle to shoulder, waited until they had moved well out of line with the girl, then squeezed the trigger. An instant after the rifle's sharp bark, a spike buck crumpled to the ground.

Carry heard the shot and came across to join him, watching as he dressed out the buck. He made quick work of it and, finished, heaved the carcass to his horse's back, roping it behind the saddle.

"There's the *Belle*," Carry told him as he was wiping his knife and hands clean on the tall grass.

He looked upriver and saw the steamer drawing out from a point of land in the near distance. "Hargutt misses his chance at those bull-heads," he said as he stepped into the saddle.

In another quarter-hour they were leading their horses back aboard the *Belle*.

Supper was over and the *Belle* lay moored to the bank, Hargutt having wisely decided not to crowd his luck in trying to navigate by this fading, tricky light. Will and Tom Knight had left Carry and Ned at their table in the saloon and, having climbed to the hurricane, were sitting on the bench up forward that Hargutt had earlier in the day pointed out to Carry and Will.

The day's heat had already gone out of the air, it was almost chilly now and would be really cold later tonight. From here they could look down and keep a watch on the wagon. Evening's lingering light lay across the wide, swollen river. Bullfrogs honked close by and off to the left along the far shore a flock of geese rose out of a swampy inlet, circled and headed into the fading purple glow of the sunset, marking a broad V against the darkening blue of the heavens. The dying glow of a fire off behind the cottonwoods along the near bank marked the spot where several of the roustabouts had gone ashore to cook supper and spend the night.

"Never tires a man's eye, this country," Tom Knight quietly remarked. "It's better in some ways than it used to be, poorer in others." He gave Will a sidelong glance. "Ever think back and wish you'd hung your hat some place else besides Crow Track, son?"

"Never."

Knight sensed the implied compliment and was pleased by it. "At least we got the country pretty well cleared of hostiles. What were the ones we saw back up the river this afternoon, Crows?"

Will shook his head. "Looked to me like Piegans. Probably a hunting party off the reservation. They let 'em do that this time of year to save on the beef issue. A dozen or so families in a bunch will move out into good country, set up their lodges and hunt till the cold drives them back in."

"Hunt what, buffalo? Poor pickin's if that's what they're after. I haven't set eyes on more than a hundred head over the last two or three years."

"Buffalo if they can find some, deer and elk if they can't."

Tom nodded matter-of-factly, not really thinking of buffalo or Piegans or Crows but of something closer to his heart. As they talked he had been studying Will's angular profile in a speculative, probing way, and now he brusquely drawled, "Every time I see you and that black-haired girl of mine together I wonder why the hell it's wound up the way it has."

That blunt remark jolted Will. His inclination was to let it pass and say nothing. Yet out of politeness and a certain wary curiosity he finally asked, "What way, Tom?"

The older man breathed a long, slow sigh. "Forget I said it. No way at all."

Will drew slowly on his pipe, wondering what strange turn Tom Knight's thinking was taking this moment. And at length, mentally shrugging aside that wonder, he asked, "Who won the toss on staying up with the wagon, you or Ned?"

"We didn't toss. Ned just up and said he'd do it." Again Knight eyed Will in that probing, half-uneasy way. "Which is what I was trying to get at. Ned. What the devil's come over the man?"

"Didn't know anything had."

"He's skittery as a mean colt. Try and talk with him. His mind's . . . Well, call it slippery. He can be sayin' one thing and you know damn wolf he's thinkin' another."

Will wasn't liking the turn their talk was taking and drawled mildly, "He's worrying about the gold in those kegs down at the wagon. And no wonder."

"That's not his worry," Knight stated flatly. "Know what I think? There's something between him and Danbo. Just now while we were eatin' I caught him when he didn't know I was watching. He was glaring at that tinhorn like he could've slit his gullet."

Just where this talk was leading mystified Will. Tom seemed to be trying to tell him something and hadn't yet worked around to the point. Sure of that, he now kept a strict silence that was shortly broken as the other burst out, "Will, I'm gettin' so I don't trust the man!"

"Danbo?"

"No, confound it, Ned!"

Hard surprise hit Will. He had instinctively been expecting something like this, yet it came as a blow to hear Tom so bluntly word his feelings. And now, before he could say anything, Tom went on, "And that's not all, not by a mile-long shot. Know what the fool kid's doing? Courtin' a woman on the side."

Something tightened inside Will. Carefully schooling his expression, smiling sparely, he drawled, "Well, what man doesn't look at more than one woman now and then?"

"Look at, hell! This is more than that I tell you."

Will shook his head. "You're dreamin', Tom. Ned never —"

"It's no dream. Old Frank Euler across in Leesville came to me a month ago about it. Frank and I have been friends since before you came along. It about cut the heart out of him to have to say it, but he decided I ought to know since the whole town did."

Will didn't often swear, yet just now he did, softly, angrily. "Tom, I don't want to hear any more. So keep it to yourself. Far as Carry's concerned, you ought not —"

"You think I'd tell her?" Knight cut in hotly. "No, never. But damn Ned for messing up her life!"

"He hasn't messed it up. And he won't."

"But he will I tell you. Why, by God, I even followed him to Leesville on one of his trips, stuck my nose in his business. I know for a fact he spent the night with that woman."

Sighing helplessly, Will leaned forward and held his head in his hands to say, "Suppose he has gone loco over Grace Drew? I still say —"

"So you've known about it?" Tom interrupted, pointedly adding, "You must've. I hadn't mentioned her name. How'd you find out?"

"Came to town to find him a couple nights

ago. He wasn't anywhere around, so I went to the yard and pried it out of one of the men. Ned had been there to get a horse."

Tom Knight shook his head savagely, asking, "Why would he do it? Why, I ask?"

"Ask him, Tom, not me."

"If I do I bust it up between him and Carry. And the last thing I'll be is a meddlin' father."

"Then let it slide, let Carry figure it out."

"How can she?"

Will straightened, eyeing the older man squarely. "Any time you think that girl's coming up with a wrong count you ought to think again. Let things ride, I say."

Tom Knight stared bleakly out across the dusk-shrouded river for all of a minute without speaking. Then, "All right, let Carry sort it out herself. But what's this between Ned and Danbo?"

"Nothing I know of."

"There's something there, I tell you. They were up there on the middle deck this morning with their heads together. Right after you and Carry left me there by the wagon. They were there a good hour, havin' it back and forth like a couple women over a back fence. And all of it wasn't friendly from what I could make out."

"Could be that Danbo's sore about having to give over his partnership in the yard."

"If that made him sore the time for him to've said it was when the three of you got together the day after you got back."

Will came up off the bench now and stepped to the edge of the deck to stare below. Two passengers, one softly playing a mouth-organ, were sitting on the tongue of the Crow Track wagon. Its tarp was still roped tightly in place. Will, having made sure of that, turned slowly to face Tom Knight.

"I'll say this much. Ned isn't the man he was two years ago. That doesn't mean he's changed for the bad; but he is different. It's hard to peg what I mean."

"With what he's doing to Carry, there's got to be a crooked streak in him."

"That'd take some proving, Tom," Will said softly. "A lot."

"Which I aim to furnish sooner or later."

There was no further point in pursuing this disagreeable subject and Will picked this moment to say, "Give the man the benefit of the doubt. Quit worryin' it around in your mind. Now suppose we talk about the weather, anything but what neither of us knows a fool thing about."

The older man's glance met Will's soberly, directly. "There's another thing you don't know, my friend." He waited out a deliberate interval before stating in typical bluntness, "That girl of mine could lose her head to you if you so much as wagged a finger at her."

Will's dark face went slack with astonishment. "That's the . . . Tom, you're a . . ."

"Quit stammerin', son." Knight's soberness

eased before a faint, knowing smile. "My eyes are mighty good. I've noticed a thing or two that could add up to something mighty fine for you and for Carry if the two of you would only let it."

He came stiffly up off the bench now, drawling, "Well, a man can keep hoping. Suppose you think over what I've said while I go keep Carry company so Ned can get down to the wagon."

Will had been sleeping quite soundly when the knifing cold air rising off the river wakened him. He rolled himself more tightly in the blanket and peered up through the railing runners at the deck's edge to look at the stars. The Great Bear told him that it was well past two of the new morning.

He shut his eyes and lay there relishing the new warmth of the blanket, trying to keep his thoughts idle, wanting to drop off to sleep again. But shortly he found himself mulling over what Tom Knight had said last evening about Ned and Carry. And the troubled run of his thoughts only brought him wider awake until presently he was casting back and remembering the many incongruities of the past several days.

The sum of all these was that Ned was a changed man. Galling as it had been to listen to Tom Knight's indictment, Will knew that Tom had no more than shrewdly voiced what he himself had been thinking, consciously or unconsciously. Ned was moody with no apparent reason for being so, he was quick to anger without any surface cause. And, mysteriously, he had either purposely or without realizing it shed a habit of long standing: that of confiding in Will.

Out of the welter of Will's speculation rose one fact which couldn't be ignored. Two of Ned's own crew had robbed the stage the other night. Worts had paid the ultimate penalty for his act, yet his dying hadn't prevented Matt Kelso from making away with enough gold to last most men half a lifetime.

How had these two men of the yard crew, and perhaps a third, known that the stage would be carrying gold? Only four men — Will, Ned, Tom and Baker at the bank — had known of the shipment. Had Worts and Kelso only played a hunch or had they actually known what was on the stage?

Will could find no sure answer to these questions. He had only a few bare facts to go on. Clyde Worts was in his grave. Matt Kelso was gone, carrying stolen gold and riding a bay horse stolen from the yard in . . .

A bay horse!

Will sat bolt upright as that casual recollection took on instant significance. The stranger he had sighted on the hunt today had been riding a bay!

It took Will but an instant to think back and be positive that the stranger's solid-looking build had strongly resembled Matt Kelso's. He was equally as positive that if the rider had been

158

Kelso the man might well have been following the *Belle.* If Kelso had known what the stage was carrying the other evening he might also know what had been loaded into the Crow Track wagon behind the bank last night.

Ridiculous as the notion seemed, Will was nonetheless awed and a trifle alarmed by the remote chance that he had stumbled upon something ominously important. He sat there another moment in doubt, wondering how he could explain the strange run of his thoughts to Ned. Then he tossed his blanket aside, pulled on his boots and came erect to hurry forward along the darkened deck.

As he rounded the corner of the forward cabin and turned toward the head of the main staircase he slowed his pace momentarily, annoyed at realizing he had left his holstered Colt's and shellbelt lying back there at the head of his blanket. But that didn't matter just now, and he hurried on to the stairway and turned down it, his boots thudding solidly against the treads.

At the foot of the steps he found the main deck so dark that he had to reach out with both hands and feel his way forward toward the wagon between the stacks of bales and crates and barrels. The night's hard chill told him that few if any of the deck passengers were spending the night out here in the open. Even last week before he had left the boat at Rock Point the nights had been so uncomfortable that passengers and crew alike had taken to sleeping in behind the stacks of cordwood where the heat from the dying fires of the boilers lessened the damp chill of the river air.

Abruptly the wagon's high shape stood vaguely outlined against the blackness close ahead, and Will called softly, "Ned!"

An instant later he caught a hint of movement in the darkness to his right. He was turning that way, thinking it was Ned, when a man's driving weight slammed into him from behind and drove him hard off his feet.

SIX

The hollow echo of a man's boot-tread striking so unexpectedly across the night's restless stillness from the direction of the stairway had made both Ned and Danbo, alongside the wagon on the *Belle*'s foredeck, wheel around in sudden apprehension.

Ned had some seconds ago awkwardly lifted the two hundred-pound kegs from the wagon bed. They now sat the deck between them near a coil of rope, some rags and a gunnysack which Danbo had brought down here intending to use in tying and gagging Ned before he carried the kegs ashore.

No sooner had Ned's glance swung toward the stairway than he made out a shadowy figure moving this way along the narrow, crooked aisle between the stacks of freight reaching back along the deck.

"It's Speer! Go stop him!"

Danbo's hushed whisper stiffened Ned in momentary panic. Then, strangely, that numbing emotion in Ned was drowned by a surge of scalding rage rising from deep within him as he recognized Will.

Until now his and Danbo's plan for taking the gold off the *Belle* had worked to perfection. Through the fortunate circumstance of this being a bitterly cold night they had the foredeck to themselves, with not a soul sleeping near by to see or hear them. The kegs were out of the wagon. All that remained to be done was for Danbo to tie and gag Ned, then carry the kegs into the willows along the bank, and their worries were over.

And now Will Speer was groping his way toward them along the night-shrouded deck.

In one instant of startling clarity, Ned Oakes saw Will as being the only thing, the only person, standing in the way of his settling his score with Danbo once and for all. In a flash of warped reasoning Will became to him the single instrument of his not having paid off that debt to the gambler three nights ago in Leesville.

Finally, and perhaps most galling of all, he suspected that Will was somehow turning Carry against him. Will and the girl had been alone together on the stage the morning after the Leesville robbery, he had himself been a witness to their lighthearted yet somehow intimate talk in the yard office after the stage's arrival. Yesterday morning Carry had obviously been eager to leave the boat with Will and ride out alone on the hunt with him. And her manner had been definitely cool and distant throughout the afternoon and evening.

His bitter realization of these glaring facts, plus the wearing strain of having had to deceive both Carry and Will these past few days, swayed Ned Oakes to act instinctively now in a way he never would have had he been completely sane. Hate was an emotion he had never before even remotely felt toward Will. Yet this moment hate blinded him beyond all reason. This, along with his unconscious fear of the man, made him reach out to clutch Lyle Danbo's arm and savagely draw the smaller man close to him.

"The sack!" he whispered. "Push it in his face when I have him down."

He shoved Danbo roughly away from him then and saw the gambler turn toward the kegs and snatch up the gunnysack. Will's shape was moving in on him as he crouched behind a waist-high crate, seeing Danbo drop from sight barely five feet opposite between two barrels beyond the gold kegs.

The scrape of Will's boots was plainly audible. The big man called softly, "Ned!" as his tall shape moved abreast the crate.

Will must have seen Danbo move an instant later, for abruptly he wheeled halfway around, putting his back to Ned. With a hard upward lunge, Ned threw his shoulder at the middle of Will's back. The big man grunted and pitched forward and down between the two barrels. His head smashed into one with a loud thud. And Ned, throwing his weight on that sprawling figure, felt Will's body go suddenly loose under him.

Lyle Danbo, the gunnysack held in both hands, fell hard across Will's head and shoulders, harshly breathing, "Get the rope!" But then, seeing that Will hadn't moved, he eased slowly back into a crouch, saying softly, gloatingly, "We're in luck. You knocked him cold."

Ned was taking no chances. He stepped quickly over to pick up the rope, came back with it and made three tight turns about the ankles of Will's boots. Having made his tie, he took a knife from his pocket, cut the rope and tossed it to Danbo, saying curtly, "Pin his arms to his sides and tie him. Hurry it!"

"What's the rush, boy?" Danbo's tone was larded with amusement. He seemed as calm and unruffled as though he sat at his poker layout in his parlor back in Rock Point.

In five more minutes Will lay completely helpless and apparently still unconscious, wrists and ankles bound. arms roped to his sides, a gag tied between his jaws. Ned was breathing heavily as he came erect and stared down into the shadows at his friend. It occurred to him suddenly that Will might well be dead, and he bent down quickly, sighing in relief when he felt the regular rise and fall of Will's wide chest.

"Now all you do is truss me up, leave me lyin' alongside him and take off with your kegs," he told Danbo, speaking very softly.

"Let's think this out." Over a brief pause the gambler went on, "If you're found lying here in the morning, and if Speer and the gold are both gone, what's everyone going to think?"

Ned stood motionless a moment as he digested what he had heard. Then, "What's to happen to Will?"

"Simple enough. This man I have waiting for me off there in the brush'll take him along for a day or so. When he's far enough away, he turns Speer loose. On foot. By the time Speer finds his way back to some ranch or town, my man's disappeared and Speer has to do some tall talkin' to clear himself. If he can clear himself."

The man's cool logic made sense. Ned had but one small remaining doubt. And now Danbo, as though having read his mind, stated softly, "Nothing for you to worry about. You were lyin' here hit over the head and all trussed up. Speer can give any story he likes about what happened and you don't have to know a thing. You didn't see who hit you any more than he did."

Ned nodded at once. "Then let's get it done."

Several years ago no river captain would have risked tying up for the night in this country without putting guards ashore and holding his boat well clear of the bank with spars, for the Cheyenne and the Sioux were a constant menace along the upper Missouri. But this fall, especially this far below the Musselshell, that danger no longer threatened. Joseph and his Nez Perces, the only remaining warring tribe, were to busy outriding the cavalry far to the west to represent any danger.

Tonight, in fact, several roustabouts were sleeping near a fire under the cottonwoods a good two hundred yards away. And the staging plank was in place, its outer end lying securely on the bank.

They carried Will ashore and lugged his inert weight off through the willows to a clear stretch of open ground in a direction opposite that of the fire's feeble glow. "This'll do," Danbo finally said, and they eased their burden to the ground.

"Now we get back there, truss you up, I lug the kegs across here and it's done."

Ned wasn't forgetting something that had been rankling since his talk with the gambler alongside the levee back at Rock Point, and he asked tartly, "How's Kelso going to find you when you get back here?"

"Kelso?" the gambler echoed blandly, shaking his head. "Man, won't you ever learn to trust me?"

"No."

Danbo sighed deeply. "Later on you'll maybe know how wrong you've been. But for now you're square with me. You don't owe me another thing."

Ned's heady relief at hearing these words outweighed his distrust of the man. For the first time in many, many weeks he felt the burden of worry and constant apprehension easing from his mind. Only one thing remained to be settled between him and Danbo, and now he glanced down at Will's outstretched form to say tonelessly, "Lyle, Will's knocked out. But he's alive and nothing's wrong with him. If anything happens to him from now on you're going to answer to me for it."

"Nothing will happen to him."

Danbo reached out then and took Ned by the arm, saying, "Let's get at it."

Carry was wakened early the next morning by her father shaking her by the shoulder. She looked up at him with a drowsy smile, then came wider awake as she took in the severe set of his hawkish face.

Pushing quickly up on an elbow, her ebony hair falling down across one shoulder, she said knowingly, "Something's wrong, Tom!"

"Afraid there is."

He began tersely telling her what had happened. One of the roustabouts had found Ned lying bound and gagged under the wagon down on the main deck shortly before sunrise, just after Hargutt had given the orders for the *Belle*'s hawsers to be taken in in preparation for getting the boat under way. Tom himself, having risen early, had reached the main deck just as they were cutting the ropes from Ned's arms and legs.

During the latter hours of the night someone Ned hadn't seen or even heard had crept up behind him, struck him a hard blow along the side of his face and knocked him unconscious. His face was cut and swollen, badly bruised.

Carry, who had listened in spellbound amazement, let Tom get this far in his story when she

167

asked, "But why was Ned down there by the wagon?"

Tom told her, told her about the kegs containing upward of fifty thousand dollars in gold, the bank's gold. The kegs were gone. At the girl's look of mute incredulity, he explained, "We didn't want you to know about it, didn't want you to have to worry over it. Only Baker and me and Will and Ned knew it was —"

"Then that's why the three of you loafed down there so much yesterday," she cut in.

He nodded sparely and then solemnly stated, "But there's more to this. We've searched the boat high and low. We can't find Will."

Carry came bolt upright on the bed, her dark eyes showing such strong alarm that Tom hastened to say, "Now don't get upset. Any one of a dozen things could've happened. Will probably got up with the chickens and walked off the boat for a look around —"

"But wouldn't he have gone to the wagon first to see Ned?"

Knight sighed wearily, worriedly, answering with a reluctant nod. "That's what gets me. Can't begin to understand it. But . . . Well, anyway he's gone and we've got to find him."

He sat on the bed's edge. "Look, girl. We've told Hargutt about the gold. But no one else is to know. We've let the story get out that a couple rifles and a case of ammunition's missing from the wagon. Hargutt's one prime gent. He's keeping the boat right where she is until Ned and

168

I have the chance to ride out for a look around. If we aren't back by say ten o'clock, he's moving up the river four or five miles and putting his crew ashore to cut more firewood. Come evening he'll drop back down here again to spend the night."

Carry pushed him away and swung her feet from beneath the blankets. "I'm going with you."

"You're not. You'll stay right here." The unnatural severity of his tone did more than anything to drive home to her the seriousness of this thing. "If you went along with us someone might get the notion that there's more to this than we're telling. And we don't want that."

"But what could have happened to Will?"

The near-desperation of her glance made him shake his head almost savagely. He wasn't enough of an actor to deceive her and answered honestly, "It's got me whipped. We found his blankets and gun out on deck. My guess, for what it's worth, is that he may have got up and gone down for a look at the wagon sometime during the night. Whoever slugged Ned may have . . ." With a helpless shrug, he added tartly, "I just don't know."

Carry rose to stand beside him now, saying gravely, "The gold, Tom. Unless you can find it you . . . you and the bank are in real trouble, aren't you?"

"The gold?" He lifted a hand and ran it across his forehead, laughing uneasily. "Funny, but I haven't thought much about that end of it. It's Will I'm thinkin' of."

The weary sag of his shoulders as he turned toward the door now made Carry quickly say, "Tom, remember one thing. Will can look out for himself. If he's in trouble, he'll get out of it. If he isn't . . . Well, he may show up any minute."

"That's too much to hope for."

She walked to the door of the cabin with him, asking, "Where's Ned?"

"Back in the kitchen soaking the side of his face with hot water. We're going to grab a bite there and be on our way."

"If I hurry and dress can I see him before you go?"

"Yes, if you hurry."

As she dressed Carry's imagination ran wild, deepening the alarm she felt over Will's strange disappearance. Oddly enough she gave no more than a passing thought to Ned. It was, therefore, something of a shock to her when, leaving her cabin, she met her father and Ned coming from the kitchen along the aisle between the tables.

Ned made a thoroughly convincing victim. Danbo, after tying and gagging him last night, had hit him such an unexpectedly vicious blow that he had been dazed, close to unconsciousness. The gambler's heavy signet ring had cut a two-inch gash high along the cheekbone under his right eye. That side of his face was lividly bruised and so swollen that he had the look of having a generous cut of plug tobacco stuffed in his cheek.

"Ned, that cut!" Carry cried softly as she came up to him.

"Looks worse than it feels." He gave her a rueful smile. "Leave it to me to make a mess of things."

"But how could you help it if you didn't even hear this . . . Who could it possibly have been?"

Tom, standing impatiently alongside Ned, answered gruffly, "Probably someone that'd been following the boat ever since we left Rock Point. We may come across his tracks. You ready, Ned?"

Ned answered with a nod, and the three of them walked the length of the saloon and out to the main stairway where Tom paused long enough to tell Carry, "Better stay up here, girl. And remember, we lost a pair of rifles and a case of shells, nothing more."

"But people are going to ask about Will, Tom."

"Then tell 'em he made off with the rifles and shells."

Ned eyed the older man in a frowning, probing way to ask, "So you've thought of it, too?"

"Thought of what?"

"That Will took the gold."

A look of scorn and loathing instantly hardened Tom Knight's expression. "I've been waiting for this," he said, very softly. "Waiting and wondering how long it'd take you to try and saddle it all on to Will. Now that you have suppose you stay right where you are while I have a go at this alone."

He gave Ned no chance at all to make amends, but turned away at once and disappeared down the stairway to the deck below. And Ned, finally recovering from his surprise, found the voice to ask amazedly, "What brought that on, Carry? I only said —"

"I heard what you said," she cut in, the chill in her tone conveying even more scorn than her father's had a moment ago. "You meant it, too. You could really believe such a thing of Will."

"But the gold's gone! I only tried to —"

"Don't, Ned!" Once again she cut him short. And now as his face took on a ruddy flush at the pointedness of her accusing stare, his glance wavered and fell away. It was then that she told him, "We won't talk about it. But you know what this must mean for the two of us. Now will you please go away and let me try and forget that Will ever called you his friend."

"Carry, I swear I was only . . . was trying to . . ."

She had turned her back on him and walked away as he was speaking. And now as she strode out into the bright sunlight to stand alone at the rail, Ned Oakes knew that he had lost her.

Will Speer's awareness came slowly alive with the hard chill of the dawn hour. For quite an interval he vaguely realized he was hanging belly-

172

down behind the withers of a horse ahead of a tarp-covered pack, that his wrists and boots were bound together under the horse's barrel.

His head pounded savagely with a deep aching. He wanted to cry out but couldn't summon the strength. A growing conviction that he must be badly hurt finally penetrated his wandering, pain-numbed thoughts. He opened his eyes and for some minutes stared sightlessly down at the sandy soil, the clumps of grass and weeds passing below. Finally he managed to turn his head and see that his horse was being led by a rider whose broad back swayed in lazy rhythm to the motion of the second animal, a bay.

All this confounded him and over the torment of his throbbing brain he tried to recall something that would explain his being here. Then presently it came back to him.

He had been walking the *Belle*'s darkened lower deck toward the wagon in search of Ned sometime during the night. There had been something he had wanted Ned to know. What that was he couldn't now recall, though he could clearly remember that he had been close to the wagon when suddenly he had been knocked off his feet and head-first into some object that must have been a great deal harder than his skull.

Mulling this over, he was unexpectedly jarred hard by his horse stumbling. The fierce stab of pain knifing through his brain made him groan in agony and close his eyes. A few seconds later he felt the horse stop. And then a gruff voice was saying cheerily, "So you come to."

He opened his eyes and weakly lifted his head to see Matt Kelso stepping out of the saddle of the animal up ahead. And in that split second he knew what it was he had wanted to tell Ned last night.

Kelso dropped his reins and sauntered on back to stand alongside Will's horse. "Got to hand it to you, Speer. You take a worse beatin' than a mule. Want to get down and stretch?"

He laughed at Will's feeble nod. Then Will could feel him fumbling with the rope on the far side of the horse. Abruptly Will's hands came free and he found he could bend his knees. He reached up, caught a hold on the horse's mane and lifted his upper body so that he slid off the animal's back.

Kelso caught him as his knees buckled, eased him to a sitting position on the ground, then stepped back to stare down at him. "How's the head?"

Will ignored the question, relishing the easing of the pain in his brain. And shortly he was able to look up at Kelso and ask, "Why'd you have me trussed up?"

"Why?" The question seemed to puzzle Kelso. "You don't know?"

Will shook his head, whereupon the other stepped over to his horse to lay a hand on one of a pair of bulging pouches below the bedroll tied to the cantle of his saddle. "This here's gold,

Speer. There's more in that pack on the nag you're ridin'. The gold out of them kegs that were aboard Knight's wagon. You're missin' along with it. When they put two and two together, who'll they think made off with it?"

The shock of discovering that Kelso had stolen the gold from Crow Track's wagon penetrated Will's numbed consciousness like a knife-thrust. He was awed and alarmed when he tried to think of what this would mean to Tom Knight, and to the bank. But Kelso's last remark bore an even more ominous quality.

He, Will Speer, was alone responsible for the gold having been brought down the river. Now the gold had been stolen off the *Belle* and, as Kelso had just reminded him, he had disappeared from the boat along with it. Either knowingly or by accident, Kelso had managed it so that suspicion would surely fall on him.

Will closed his eyes as this bleak awareness came over him. And his voice was hollow, lifeless as he asked, "So what do you do with me?"

Kelso laughed. "Only one thing to do. If you never show up, and if the gold don't neither, then what're people going to think?"

When Will made no answer, Kelso supplied his own. "Just what they're supposed to. You knocked your partner in the head, tied him up and robbed the wagon."

Will held his head in his hands, for some strange reason feeling quite unmoved by what he had heard. *If you never show up, and if the gold don't neither . . .*

What Kelso intended doing with him was quite obvious. Sometime today, or perhaps not until tomorrow, the man would use either the handgun he was wearing or the Winchester on his saddle. A shot sounding across this empty land would probably never be heard by human ear. Nor would a caved-in cutbank ever be recognized as a grave. Kelso, he knew, was thoroughly capable of cold-blooded murder.

As the realization that Kelso intended killing him sank home, a question came to Will's mind. The answer to it didn't really matter, but he voiced it anyway. "You haven't been in much of a hurry. How come? Won't anyone be chasin' us?"

"Sure they will. Way the hell and gone off east, if they haven't give up a'ready. We rode the bed of a creek away from the river for two hours, then doubled back a ways over rocky ground. We're headed west up the river where they won't think to look for us."

Kelso sauntered over to his horse now and came back carrying a canteen which he handed across. Will drank swallow after swallow until he had to pause to catch his breath, and then drank more. His thirst finally quenched, he upended the canteen over his head, sighing in blissful relief as the water's coolness eased the feverish throbbing in his brain.

When he finally handed the near-empty canteen back to Kelso the man slapped the holster he wore along his thigh, saying curtly, "You'll

176

take the lead from here on so's I can keep an eye on you. One slip and I use this. Now climb aboard and I'll tie you on."

Presently they moved on again, Will pointing the way at a steady jog according to Kelso's, "Keep the sun at your back." Kelso had made his prisoner fairly comfortable, boots loosely but securely roped under the horse's belly so that he could lean against the pack for support. And he had left Will's arms and hands free.

Now that he could think more rationally, other questions came to Will that cried out for answers. How, for instance, had Matt Kelso known about the gold in the Crow Track wagon? At first it seemed plausible that he might accidentally have seen the wagon being loaded behind the bank the other night. But then, remembering that the man was being hunted for the Leesville robbery, Will doubted he would have dared risk riding the streets of Rock Point even at the late hour the wagon had been loaded aboard the *Belle*.

In the end Will became certain that someone must have passed the word about the gold to Kelso, for the man had played something more than a mere hunch in so doggedly following the boat down the river. Only four people, Will included, had known what was in the wagon. It was absurd to think that either Tom Knight or Baker would have wanted to lose the gold they were shipping. For his own part, he knew that he hadn't by so much as a single word or look given it away that the wagon was loaded with anything but supplies for Tom Knight's horse ranch.

Ned then?

Ned?

One instant the notion seemed utterly ridiculous. But the next it didn't; for he was remembering fragments of Tom Knight's bitter remarks about Ned last evening up there on the *Belle*'s hurricane, remembering Carry's and his own concern over the man's strange behavior of the past week.

It wasn't in his makeup to tolerate such a serious doubt as this, to let it go unanswered. He had to know about Ned and Matt Kelso was his only way of knowing.

He turned awkwardly around now and glanced back at Kelso, the move making his head start to pound once more. Without thinking out exactly what he was to say, he drawled, "Were you there at the wagon last night to help Ned? Or did he tackle me alone?"

Kelso's naked look of outright guilt was eloquent and damning even though his expression turned quickly indignant. "What the hell kind of guff you trying to hand me, Speer?"

The man's blustery protest was such a patently hollow sham as to be laughable. Here, then, was evidence that Ned had helped Kelso rob the wagon.

As Will faced around again he felt completely drained of all emotion. Somehow the discovery he had made left him without surprise. It was as

178

though he had expended all his loyalty toward Ned in defending him over the past several days; as though now that he could see him for what he really was there was nothing more he could give or even wanted to give.

Ned had betrayed Tom Knight, had very possibly ruined him. He had betrayed Carry long ago in making those furtive rides to Leesville to call on Grace Drew. Lastly — and in Will's view the least important — he had betrayed his closest friend.

"Come on, you!" Kelso bridled now. "What d'you mean, ringin' Ned in on this?"

Will turned and looked back at the man. "I heard him, heard his voice before I went under," he blandly lied.

Matt Kelso's face reddened. He was anything but quick-witted and he studied Will closely in a near-puzzled way, wondering whether or not to believe what he had heard. Then finally he was convinced, and with a lift of the shoulders said, "Who cares if you know? You won't be tellin' nobody."

Here, once again, came that bald threat of Will never finishing this ride. Will paid it little attention. Instead he was thinking that the pattern of Ned's treachery was complete except for its minor details.

He eased around once more and sat staring vacantly ahead, fighting a dizziness and a nausea brought on by his strained position of the past quarter-minute. He realized now that Ned must

179

have arranged the robbing of the stage in Leesville just as he had probably rigged the robbing of one of his stages the previous week. It was bewildering to know that the man's unaccountable greed had driven him to taking such risks in deceiving those closest to him.

Over the next mile as he held his animal to a steady jog and thought back upon other things that pointed to Ned's guilt, Will gradually became more aware of his surroundings. The sun had already taken the night's chill from the air, it would be a hot day. They were riding across a series of low hummocks bare of any vegetation except for lush grass and an occasional clump of oak brush or a stunted cottonwood. Off to the north at a distance of four or five miles he could see a line of willows and taller cottonwoods he supposed marked the course of the river.

For a considerable length of time he tried to ignore his aching head and think out some way of tricking Kelso, of perhaps working the ropes free from his legs and making a run for it. But the longer he considered that possibility the more remote it became. Kelso was riding the best horse and he was probably looking for an excuse to use a bullet on his prisoner.

Presently, from beyond a rise in the direction of the river, Will noticed a flock of crows and magpies wheeling low over the ground. The crows were cawing angrily, a few of them diving groundward as though fighting a treed owl. Then shortly he saw a pair of much larger birds soar above the line of the horizon and settle back out of sight again. They were bald eagles, and he supposed they were feeding on the carcass of some animal.

He had covered perhaps another quarter of a mile when suddenly, because of his time-trained habit of always scanning the ground, he noticed something that took his hard attention. Off to his right were two deep lines gouged in the gravelly topsoil, along with the hoof marks of an unshod horse.

Swinging gradually to the right so as not to attract Kelso's attention, he took a closer look. And before he angled away once more he had seen several dried droplets of blood mixed with the sign.

All this carried its plain meaning to him. He had seen it many, many times before. An Indian riding a pony and dragging a loaded travois had passed along here within the last hour or two. Remembering the flock of crows and the two eagles he had seen a few minutes ago, he supposed that the Indian had killed a deer or an elk back there and, having thrown away the offal and dressed out his meat, was taking it to his camp.

Suddenly he remembered the Piegans he and Tom Knight had seen up the river late yesterday afternoon.

And now a faint rise of hope crowded out his disheartenment as he realized what he might do if his luck held out. He would have to be very,

181

very careful. Most important of all, he would have to hold Kelso's attention.

Once again he cocked his high frame around on the horse's bony back, saying, "Spell it out for me, Kelso. Ned passed you the word on what our rig was hauling to Leesville the other afternoon. How?"

"Never you mind how," came Kelso's surly answer. His look hardened then and he added, "Wish Clyde could be here to see how this is winding up for you."

"You and Worts were partners?"

"We were. Since years back. And damn your soul for what you did to him."

"What would you have done if someone had slugged you and you heard him making off with that gold? I fired at a sound, nothing more."

"Yeah? Well, you cut down the best sidekick I ever had."

"Those are the chances you take in the game you were playing." Will leaned back and braced an arm against his animal's hip to relieve his cramped position. The aching in his head had eased off now to a dull steady throbbing as he tried to think of a way of leading up to something he had to know about Kelso.

Shortly he thought he knew how he might do this and asked, "Where'd you two hail from before you hit Rock Point?"

Kelso scowled in trying to understand where this line of talk might be leading. He was wary and suspicious as he growled, "What's it to you?"

Will shrugged. "Just wondered. From something Ned said I had the two of you pegged as being reservation agency men."

"Me and Clyde?" Kelso laughed loudly in genuine amusement. "You pegged us wrong, mister. Them tramps that work the reservations can't find nothing better to do. Besides, the less I see of them red devils the better. Which is the prime reason I quit ridin' jobs and took to livin' in towns. Went through one Indian scare once and that was enough."

"You don't talk their lingo?"

"Why the hell should I want to?"

Will schooled his expression to one of strict soberness, trying not to show the satisfaction he was taking from having pried this admission from Kelso. It might be unimportant; yet as he glanced lazily beyond the man now to see the line of the travois marks still showing plainly some thirty or forty yards away, he was much relieved at knowing Kelso must be fairly ignorant of the ways of Indians. The man probably wouldn't know what the sign meant even if he should happen to notice it.

Still, Will was taking no chances. He was keeping his distance from the sign while at the same time riding parallel to it as he once again peered at Kelso to ask, "What would you be thinking of Worts if he'd crossed you the way Ned did me?"

"He never would've, not Clyde."

"Never thought Ned would've either. But I

183

should have known, the way he was playing both ends to the middle with the Knight girl."

Kelso's look took on a tinge of disgust. "Some of the boys were making a play for Grace Drew even back when Drew was alive, so Ned ain't got nothin' special there. Never could figure that gent, not since the first day I hired on. He'd gamble with women the same as he would with a card deck. With women he was lucky. Only with cards he didn't get away with it."

Here was something Will hadn't known. Yet he hid his surprise, blandly saying, "So he told me." Then, so as to sound more convincing, he added, "Fact is, he claims he damn near lost his shirt."

"Don't think he didn't. Why, a month or two back he owed Danbo close to . . ."

Kelso abruptly checked his words, making Will immediately sense that the man had come very close to saying something he hadn't intended. That something obviously had to do with Lyle Danbo.

And now, wondering what it might be, Will nodded as casually as he could. "He told me about that, too."

"The hell he did." Kelso was plainly surprised.

"Didn't he say he lost to the tune of five thousand?"

Will's question was based on a completely blind guess. He chose the figure five thousand because that had been the amount of Danbo's investment in the partnership with Ned. And he knew immediately from the way Kelso's look turned impassive so quickly that he had touched very accurately upon something he wasn't supposed to know.

"Never did find out what he owed Danbo," came Kelso's wary answer.

Quite suddenly Will was recalling a thing that had baffled him for the past several days. No sooner had it come to mind than he was voicing it. "There was a third man back in the alley at Leesville with you the other night. Who was he?"

"Wasn't no third man." Kelso's reply came too quickly, too positively. "Just me and Clyde."

"You took along a spare jughead then?"

"Yeah, a spare."

"Who else was with you?" Will insisted. "Another man from the yard?"

"Go soak your sore head, Speer. I tell you there wasn't no other man."

This line of talk, so seemingly promising a moment ago, had run into a dead end, Will decided. Kelso was through talking, or if he wasn't . . .

Danbo!

The thought struck Will with such force and conviction that it made him laugh aloud to think how blind he'd been. Kelso, startled by his outburst, growled, "What's so damned funny?"

"My bein' so thickheaded. It took me too long to see it."

"See what?"

"Who the third man was."

185

Matt Kelso's glance narrowed suspiciously. "Told you there wasn't no third man."

"But there was. It was Danbo."

For the second time over this past half-hour that telltale flush mounted to Kelso's square face. He was on the point of saying something when Will cut him short. "Ned and Danbo both rigged it to have their stages stopped. Ned was in hock to Danbo and that was his way of paying off. What you're carrying right now is part of the payoff. Danbo must've helped Ned jump me last night."

"That bump on the head busted your brains loose, Speer. Now sit back around and move that nag on faster. And no more of that hog-wash."

Kelso meant what he said. His look had turned ugly. And Will, pushing his animal on at a quicker gait, could presently begin to understand what had made Ned behave so strangely the past several days. Somehow — he might never know the real facts — Danbo's hold on Ned had driven the man to this final desperate betrayal.

And now Lyle Danbo took on a new personality in Will's eye. The man must be very shrewd, very calculating and not at all the gentleman gambler he appeared to be.

Will's preoccupation as he thought all this out had made him forget the sign he had been so carefully following. All at once remembering it, he looked off to his right down a gentle slope they were traversing. The travois marks weren't there.

He anxiously studied the broken ground beyond the foot of the slope, deciding finally that it was too rough for any hope of it holding the sign he was looking for. A weighty discouragement was settling through him then as his glance shuttled ahead once more. He had lost the one chance that had given him any hope whatsoever of outwitting Matt Kelso.

For all of a minute he sat staring vacantly ahead, thinking of what the day was to bring. That bleak prospect held no terror for him, he was instead seeing it as it related to Carry and Tom Knight, and to Ned and Danbo. His sharpest regret came when he realized how completely Carry had been deceived. But then, thinking back on what the girl had said of Ned, he guessed that her intuition would probably save her from making a mistake she might regret for the rest of her life.

He idly noticed that the river cottonwoods were closer than they had been, not over a mile distant. Presently they would have to angle to the south to avoid meeting . . .

Suddenly he was really seeing something he had been staring at sightlessly for a considerable interval. It was a faint blue haze of woodsmoke hanging against the pale backdrop of the trees off there.

For the first time since he had regained consciousness, he completely forgot the throbbing of his head as a strong excitement lifted in him. He rode across an open stretch of ground and then, a brushy rise hiding that veil of smoke, he angled slightly in the direction of the river. He covered the next half mile without sighting the trees again. Then as the ground to the north flattened out he glimpsed the smoke once more.

It was much closer than he had realized it would be, scarcely a quarter of a mile distant. And now he urged his animal on at a faster gait, heading for a twisting coulee that would put them out of sight of the smoke. As he finally rode down into the shallow depression and saw that its course swung gently riverward, every muscle in him tightened in anticipation. If he could manage to follow the coulee to its end without Kelso calling for a change in direction, and if the smoke meant what he thought it did, he might once more have the chance he had so carefully been trying for.

Suddenly from behind him Kelso bawled, "God A'mighty, look off there!"

Will swung around. Kelso lifted an arm to point to the south and obliquely to the rear in a direction opposite that of the river. Two mounted Indians, naked to the waist, were watching them from the rim of the coulee some three hundred yards away. Each of them — Will at once knew them to be Piegans — held a rifle slanted across his animal's withers.

Kelso, panicked, raked his horse with spurs and drew alongside Will, asking hoarsely,

"What're they after? What'll we do?"

Will tried to appear alarmed. "We keep going straight ahead. And easy. If you let on like you're scared we could lose our scalps."

Kelso's stare was one of naked fear. And here, thought Will, was the final proof of the man's ignorance. For Piegans were known to be a peaceful clan, no one of them would dare lay hand on a white man in this country. They had long ago become docile and resigned to reservation life.

Will kept steadily on along the bottom of the coulee. In several more moments, with Kelso riding alongside him and constantly looking to the rear, he had a thought that made him say tersely, "If it comes to a showdown it'll be you alone against the two of them. How about letting me have your Colt's?"

"And have you blow a hole through me?" Kelso laughed, his tone edged with hysteria.

"Then take the shells out and let me have it. The least we can do is run a bluff when they come at us."

Kelso sat a long moment thinking this out. Then abruptly he reached down and drew his .44 from holster. His hands were shaking as he rocked open the weapon's loading gate and punched out the shells.

He was handing Will the holstered gun and heavy shell belt when Will said, "If they see me roped to this jughead they'll know they've got only one man to fight. Better cut me loose."

189

Suspicion at once tinged Kelso's glance. But his alarm evidently outweighed his mistrust of Will, for the next moment he reached into pocket, brought out a clasp knife and, opening its big blade, bent low in the saddle to reach down and hack at the ropes that bound Will's boots together under his horse's barrel.

For an instant Will thought he might reach down and club the man alongside the head with the .44. But Kelso moved so quickly that he missed the chance as the rope fell away.

"Try anything on me and you'll be as dead as Clyde is," Kelso growled as he settled back onto the saddle. "Now get a move on and head out of here."

They rode straight on along the coulee at a steady jog. Reaching the end of the shallow depression they climbed toward open ground.

Will happened to be looking at Kelso as they topped the rise. He saw the man's face all at once go slack, saw the color drain from it.

"Look!"

Kelso's hoarse word made Will glance quickly ahead.

There, not two hundred yards away, lay the Piegan camp.

SEVEN

A quiet surge of elation and thankfulness gripped Will Speer as he eyed the four tall Piegan lodges sitting at the margin of the river cottonwoods.

He could see three squaws working at a fire between the two nearest lodges. And suddenly now several dogs off there started yapping furiously. Two of them ran this way, the hair along their backs bristling.

"Let's run for it!"

Matt Kelso was reining his bay horse hard around when Will sharply told him, "Do that and our friends back there'll cut you down."

His words made Kelso roughly haul his animal to a stand. Here was the moment that would decide this one way or the other, the moment Will had been gambling for over the past three quarters of an hour.

"If we have luck we could bluff our way out," he said.

"How?"

"Can't tell exactly yet. But I speak their lingo."

Will glanced back up the coulee to see the two braves who had been sitting their horses along the rim now advancing slowly in this direction. There was nothing unfriendly in their action.

191

They were simply curious and following a ritual that invariably marked the approach of strangers to their camp, though Will realized that to Kelso it must seem that the two had cut off their chances of retreat.

So were the squaws curious, for they had now stopped whatever they had been doing at the fire and were peering this way.

"We ride straight in," Will drawled. "Just like we owned the damn place."

"Not me, brother!"

Kelso had no sooner spoken than he was reaching out to draw his Winchester from its scabbard.

"Don't!"

Matt Kelso's hand froze within finger-spread of the rifle's stock as Will spoke that sharp word.

"Want a bullet in the back?" Will asked roughly. "Get this, Kelso. Lay a hand on that rifle and we're good as done for. Now come along. We go straight on in like I said."

He led the way on past Kelso toward the lodges, seeing that two men had joined the women. They were naked except for breech-clouts; they were unarmed. And Kelso, drawing alongside him, breathed in alarm, "There's two more bucks! Let's make a break for it before it's too late."

"Back into those two behind us? Hunh-uh! Our only chance is to try and bull this through. And don't let on you're scared."

Kelso swore soundly but made no further

move to fall behind. In a few more seconds Will was reining his animal to a stand some thirty feet short of the fire as he impassively surveyed the squaws and the two men — and three small naked children who had run from the nearest lodge — standing on the far side of the blaze.

He ignored the yapping of the dogs and lifted right hand palm outward in the traditional sign of friendliness, noticing a swarm of flies buzzing along the line of a rope strung between two saplings behind the first two lodges. Slices of drying meat hung on the rope, which was high enough to be beyond reach of the dogs.

Speaking the language of these people, he asked, "The hunt goes well?"

The nearest of the men, graying and aged, nodded in understanding. He was thin as a rail, though his stomach was round and protruding. "The hunt goes well," he answered. "The spirits smile on us. Not in many moons have we feasted so much."

The dogs had quieted and wandered off to a pile of bones beyond the fire. Will noticed that as he asked, "The white man knows you are off the reservation?"

"The white man knows. He gave us guns and powder. All the summer he sell the beef while our women and children eat flour and corn and berries. Now we are eleven mouths fewer for him to feed so long as we can hunt."

"You hunt with the long gun?"

At the man's answering nod, Will curtly told

him, "Let me see your long guns."

The Piegan was puzzled and said humbly, "The guns are old and poor. There are times when they do not shoot —"

"We look for stolen long guns, the ones of many thunders," Will cut in, raising his voice angrily. "Go! Let me see your long guns."

"There is only one among us. There are two more behind you with Walks-On-Snake and Lame Bear."

"Then show me your one long gun."

The old man turned away at once and jogged over to disappear inside the second lodge. And Kelso, who had been warily listening and watching, asked, "What does he say?"

Before answering, Will turned and peered back to see the two mounted Piegans patiently sitting their horses some fifty yards away. "He wants to know why we ride through their country spookin' away the game."

"Sore at us?"

"Plenty. If you don't think so, take a look back there."

Kelso glanced furtively to the rear and when he faced around again stark fear was once more strongly etched on his rough features. Seeing that, Will soberly told him, "Make one wrong move and we're done for."

This moment the old man reappeared from the lodge. He carried a long-barreled, heavy Sharps rifle. Its stock had been broken and was held together by windings of brass wire. It was one of the old single-shot buffalo guns intended to be used with a pole, or rod, steadying its muzzle end.

As the old man came toward them, Will drawled, "Stay set now," and unexpectedly slid off his horse to the ground.

His back muscles were knotted at the threat of Kelso being behind him as he dropped his reins and walked on around the fire to meet the aged Piegan.

The old man's glance still showed a strong puzzlement as Will paced toward him. But he was wanting to oblige as he lifted the Sharps and said, "It is rusty and old. We do not use it."

"You have other guns hidden in your lodges. Guns of many thunders." Will's tone was brusque as he referred to the repeating rifles, like Kelso's, that were so highly prized by all plains Indians.

Indignation tightened the old man's lined face. "I am a man of truth. I swear by my father's spirit and the spirit of my oldest son that this is our only other long gun."

Will could feel his pulse begin pounding in his head as, standing with his back to the threat of the Winchester, he prayed that the old man's fierce look would keep Kelso cowed and afraid to move a muscle.

He held out his hands, scowling severely, "Let me see the gun."

The Piegan didn't move for a long moment. Then, hesitantly and half afraid, he offered the Sharps.

Will roughly snatched the rifle from his hands and, drawing back its hammer, wheeled around and lifted the weapon to shoulder, staring over its sights at Matt Kelso's face gone slack with amazement.

"Reach, Kelso!"

Kelso's face purpled in rage as he saw how he had been taken in. His jaw muscles tightened and for an instant Will thought he was going to make a try for the Winchester.

But the odds were against Matt Kelso. The persuasive power of the Sharps's big bore lined so squarely at him finally decided this. He let go the reins and, very slowly, lifted his hands outward and upward.

And Will, knowing he held an empty gun, came quickly around the fire ignoring the guttural, excited talk of the Piegan squaws.

He didn't let his breath go until, alongside Kelso's horse, he had reached up and drawn the Winchester from its boot.

Tom Knight returned to the spot along the river where the *Belle* had tied up for the night some five hours after he had left the packet to ride out in search of some trace of Will Speer. And, as he had expected, the stern-wheeler was gone, having moved upriver to load wood as Hargutt had earlier agreed he would do.

The prospect of having to spend the next five or six hours idling here while he awaited the packet's return didn't appeal to Knight. He was too worried, too restless to relish the prospect of loafing. So he left the river behind him and rode straight into the south for perhaps two miles, a distance he judged would take him beyond reach of the many inlets and swamps, before swinging west to follow the distant line of cottonwoods and willows marking the big stream's twisting course.

It was at about this time that Will Speer left the Piegan camp with Kelso securely roped to his horse.

Knight had had what amounted to no luck at all in his search for any trace of Will. He had made one discovery deep in the cottonwoods close to the spot where the *Belle* had spent the night, though without being at all certain of its having any sure bearing on Will's strange disappearance. What he had found were his two missing kegs, empty, lying in the brush, and two sets of fresh hoofprints that led him as far as the bank of a shallow creek half a mile to the east downriver.

He had been excited and wary on discovering no trace of the sign along the creek's far bank. Turning up along the stream, he had ridden three slow miles up its meandering course searching for the lost sign along both banks. Finally a bleak and barren expanse of rocky ground stretching as far as a man could see into the south had stopped him. If two riders had intentionally hidden their sign by following the creek bed this far, it might take a man a week to discover where they had left this vast expanse of limestone wasteland.

It occurred to him that the two horsemen might have turned down the stream and into the Missouri, in which case they could easily have reached the far bank and lost themselves in the trackless region to the north. When he finally turned back, Tom Knight was as discouraged as he had ever been.

Now, in no particular hurry, he rode on, thinking back over the past several troubled days since Will Speer's return to Rock Point. The tall man's appearance from the dead, it seemed, had triggered a series of the most ominous events in all Knight's experience. Just what lay behind all this he had no way of knowing; though when he thought of Ned Oakes's indirect accusation this morning — of the man even daring to suppose Will could have had anything to do with the theft of the gold — his anger flared as swiftly as a too-full kettle coming to the boil. It wasn't in him to doubt Will Speer in the slightest degree.

Instead, he found himself doubting Ned, actually distrusting the man. Somehow, obscure though it was at the moment, he felt that Ned must be involved in what had happened aboard the *Belle* last night. He had more than his instinct to back this hunch. For Ned had offended him deeply and lost all his trust in having taken up with Grace Drew while at the same time pretending to be serious in his intentions toward Carry.

It wasn't Tom Knight's way to interfere where Carry and Ned were concerned. Nor was he so strait-laced that he couldn't halfway excuse Ned's furtive liaison. Yet when it came to Carry marrying a man of such flexible principles he knew he was somehow going to have to draw the line. How he could accomplish that without taking a flatfooted stand against Ned was beyond him just now. But he would if it came to a showdown. Meantime he hoped that Carry's instinct would warn her she had made a wrong choice.

Last evening up there on the *Belle*'s hurricane as he talked with Will he had touched upon something mighty close to his heart. Of all the men he had ever known, young men, Will Speer stood head and shoulders above the others. He had watched Will grow into manhood and he took the same pride in having shaped that growth that he did in knowing what a lovely woman Carry had become.

Thinking of the two, of Carry and Will, he could look back across the years and see how Will with his shyness had failed to interest Carry in contrast to Ned with his easy-going surface charm. It shamed him to recall that there had been a time when he himself had been deceived into being thankful that Carry seemed to choose Ned in preference to Will. Perhaps Carry and Ned and Will hadn't then realized that any choice was being made; but he had been strongly aware of it. Carry, with her Eastern schooling, had seemed more suited to a man like Ned whose manners and bearing and good looks were more subtly the gentleman's than Will's.

Now Tom Knight understood how very wrong he had been. Ned had turned out to be a weakling. In contrast, these past two years had matured Will to a surprising degree. Rough as Knight sensed those years must have been, Will had somehow come through them with a more lasting mark of being a real gentleman, of being a man, than Ned had ever possessed. There was an innate goodness and gentleness and integrity in Will that was probably beyond the understanding of anyone like Ned Oakes.

This is gettin' you nowhere, nowhere at all!

So thinking, Tom Knight tried to close his mind to these perplexing imponderables as he scanned the river horizon hoping to see either the *Belle*'s tall stacks showing over the trees or the smoke from her boilers. He was disappointed, and presently began looking up ahead as he wondered if Hargutt had taken the packet farther upriver than he had planned.

Something like two minutes later his idle glance picked out what he thought to be two riders coming toward him some two miles off to the southwest along a line of low, barren hills. At first a trifle surprised at sighting anyone riding this empty land, he presently lost interest.

But after a few more minutes his interest in the two abruptly quickened. If he was right in thinking that Will had been riding one of the pair of horses he had earlier tried to follow up the creek, there was a remote chance that Will and the second rider had struck west out of the vast wasteland that had swallowed their sign. If they had, these two might have sighted them.

It was with that faint hope that Knight now angled toward the two men in the distance, who in a few more minutes would be passing him a mile or so away. He covered a lazy half mile without being any more interested in the two than keeping them within sight.

Then suddenly he noticed that one of the pair made a high shape in the saddle. And even as he raked his horse with spur, sending the animal on at a hard run, he roared a whooping shout of delight, bawling, "Will!"

At his hail he saw the two riders stop, look this way, then turn toward him. And now at this lessened distance he knew he couldn't be mistaken. The taller of those two was Will Speer.

He came riding up on Will and Kelso with his hawkish face slack in amazement and delight. Reining in alongside Will, he breathed incredulously, "Lord, it's good to see you, man! But who've you got here?"

"Some prison bait, Tom."

Knight took in the lengths of rawhide holding Matt Kelso's thick legs hard against the barrel of his runty horse and burst out laughing. He laughed uproariously until the tears began streaming down his cheeks. Finally sobering, he looked around at Will. "What about the gold?"

Will was riding Kelso's bay and he turned now to lay a hand on one of the pair of bulging pouches behind the bulky bedroll. "Right here, and in that pack behind Kelso. Every ounce of it, unless our friend's got some hid away somewhere."

Knight reached out impulsively to take a tight hold on Will's arm and shake it. "Will, boy! We thought . . . Hell, I don't know what we thought. Doesn't matter now. But just what the devil happened?"

Will told him, told him as much as he knew and everything he'd guessed. And as he finished Tom Knight's stony glance settled on Kelso.

"Is this true, Kelso? About Ned and Danbo?"

"Not one damn word! He's talkin' through his hat."

A slow, chill smile touched Knight's hawkish face. He looked around at Will. "Ever try beatin' the truth out of a man, Will? Or did you ever try buildin' a grass fire and roastin' his toes till he'd talk?"

"Never did, Tom."

"Then you might as well learn how right now." Knight stepped stiffly from the saddle, motioning Will to join him as he stooped and began pulling handfuls of the long, tufted grama grass near by. "So Danbo and Ned didn't have a thing to do with it, eh, Kelso?"

"I tell you he cooked it up by himself," Kelso blustered. "I never said it was them two."

"You will, man. About two minutes from now!"

Lyle Danbo, lying in his bed in his cabin, had heard the commotion down on the main deck shortly after sunrise and had rightly assumed that it had to do with Ned and what was missing from Crow Track's wagon. He had smiled, turned over and dropped off to sleep again.

He didn't appear from his cabin until the middle of the morning, far too late for breakfast. He went on back to the galley and, giving the cook half a dollar, presently ate a plentiful meal.

Some twenty minutes after finishing the second cup of coffee he was strolling the cabin deck when Hargutt moved the *Belle* out from the bank and headed back up the river. This puzzled Danbo. He was about to ask one of the other passengers about it when, walking around the forward corner of the cabins, he spied Caroline Knight sitting in a chair alone at the rail that overlooked the main deck.

" 'Morning, Miss Knight," he said pleasantly as he came up to her. He removed his hat as she turned and nodded an answer, afterward asking, "What's this we're doing, heading back where we came from?"

Carry's answer was long in coming. She first considered telling him about Ned and the wagon. But then, not liking the man, she decided on an easier way and told him, "You'd better ask Ned about it. We're moving up a few miles to load more wood."

Danbo knew when he wasn't wanted but made

the best of it by saying cheerily, "These river captains never seem to know what they're about. Wouldn't surprise me at all if it takes Hargutt a month to land me at Bismarck." He tipped his hat once more. "So I'll go find Ned."

When he did find Ned down on the main deck after a five-minute search, his first question was, "How'd it go?"

"Not bad and not good." Ned scowled at the man and lifted a hand to the swollen side of his face then to mutter, "You came close to bustin' in the side of my face, Lyle. Wasn't called for."

"They believed your story, didn't they?" At Ned's hesitant nod, Danbo added, "Then let's say it was called for. Now how'd they take it when Speer turned up missing?"

Ned told him, told about Tom Knight having gone in search of Will. Ned was plainly worried and ended by saying, "What if he tracks Will and your man? Then where'll we be?"

"If he catches up with them you may be shy a father-in-law," was Danbo's pointed answer.

"Knight may never be my father-in-law."

Danbo took this in with some surprise. "You and Caroline on the outs?"

Ned nodded. "Because I hinted that Will might have taken that stuff out of the wagon."

"Give 'em time and they won't think that's such a bad guess."

Ned's face tightened in anger. "I thought you said nothing would happen to Will."

Danbo at once saw that his cocksureness had

betrayed him. His tongue had slipped in too boldly speaking his thoughts, and now he was trapped by his glibness. Nonetheless he made the best of it by saying, "Nothing will happen to him. What I meant was that it'll look bad for him for the next few days, till he can get the word back about what happened to him."

"You damn well meant exactly what you said."

Danbo shrugged, wearily asking, "Why put the chip on your shoulder for me, Ned? Haven't we brought this thing off?"

Ned gave him a final baleful stare and turned away without an answer to walk over to the main stairway and go up it to the cabin deck.

Ned noticed Carry sitting near the rail. Though he realized she must have seen him coming up the stairway, he hurried on back along the deck and took the ladder to the hurricane where he could be alone and out of her sight. From there he watched the packet's wood crew working along the bank felling and stripping tall thinleafs. And later, when the cook's bell clanged on the deck below to announce the noon meal, he paid it no attention, not wanting to sit at the table in the saloon with Carry and run the chance of further words with her.

As the afternoon wore on, and by the time the *Belle*'s high twin stacks started smoking with the stoking of the boilers, Ned was a thoroughly miserable man. The trip to Elkton and the horse ranch no longer held the promise of being able to forget his worries and repair his damaged relations with Carry. The girl had made it plain this morning that their affair was finished. And the prospect of spending the next week or ten days with her was becoming intolerable.

Last night down there at the wagon his warped reasoning had led him to place the blame for his poor run of luck squarely on Will. This afternoon his thinking was following much the same pattern. Will was the real cause for his misunderstanding with Carry. If it hadn't been for Will he wouldn't now be in the position of having to defend himself to Carry and Tom Knight. The man had created friction since the very hour he had set foot on the levee at Rock Point. Until his unexpected appearance, Ned's affairs had gone smoothly, very well indeed.

By the time the *Belle* eased out from the bank and got under way, Ned's thinking was taking a new turn. Danbo's implication that Will wasn't to come out of this alive had several hours ago roused him to instinctive anger. Yet, thinking of that possibility now in relation to how Will had meddled so disastrously in his affairs, his rancor and bitterness drove him to the grim hope that the gambler had in fact planned it that Will was never to be seen again. If the man disappeared as completely and mysteriously as the gold that had gone with him, then the chance was practically nonexistent that he, Ned, would ever be suspect in what had happened down on the main deck last night. If that came about, then perhaps it wasn't so impossible to suppose that he and Carry might . . .

The hoarse blast of the *Belle*'s whistle cut short his sordid ruminations. He was standing near the forward edge of the hurricane. And as the whistle sent a series of short, sharp blasts echoing out over the river, he turned and walked back to the wheelhouse, seeing Hargutt standing there leaning on the whistle-cord, grinning broadly.

As he came up to the wheelhouse's open window, Hargutt took his other hand from the wheel and pointed into the south. "There they be. Your friends and one other man. Bet you ten to one Speer's turned up with that gold!"

Ned wheeled sharply about, scanning the horizon off beyond the willows along the near bank, his pulse hammering a hard alarm. He stared off across the broken hills for all of five seconds, saw nothing and finally asked, "Where? Can't see them."

"Here." Hargutt reached out of the window to hand him a foot-long brass telescope. "Off there ahead of that cap rock. They must've heard us. They're swingin' this way."

Ned snatched the glass from the man's hand and, spotting the rock formation he thought Hargutt meant, lifted the brass tube to eye. For a long moment he saw nothing but a blur in the glass. Then, holding it steadier, he suddenly made out the shapes of three riders trotting their horses directly toward him, their images so plain that he could easily make out the puffs of dust kicked up by their animals.

The three were riding abreast. Will Speer's high shape was unmistakable. He jogged along beside a bare-headed man who sat loose in the saddle, head down. Riding on the other side of that man was Tom Knight, who now lifted an arm and waved in the direction of the river in obvious answer to the *Belle*'s signal.

"Been takin' a gander off there every now and then," Hargutt said. "Now if I can find a place to touch the bank we'll have 'em aboard in short order."

Ned took this in while still peering at Will and Tom and the man riding between them. His thoughts were confused now, a cold apprehension was settling through him. Then suddenly he was seeing that third man straighten in the saddle and lift his head.

He was looking squarely at Matt Kelso.

A numbing dread settled through Ned that moment. His thoughts ran riot for long seconds before gathering rage tightened in him and let him think halfway rationally. Matt Kelso! Danbo had tricked him. Kelso was Danbo's man and Kelso hadn't left the country after the Leesville robbery after all. Which meant . . .

A coolness threaded Ned's nerves as he turned and handed the glass to Hargutt. "I'll take the word down to the others," he said. "How long'll it be?"

"To pick 'em up?" Hargutt shrugged. "They'll

be anyway ten minutes gettin' here. It'll take me that long to find slack water and tie to the bank."

Ned turned quickly away toward the ladder leading below. Reaching the cabin deck, he hurried along it to the lounge's forward entrance, swung through it and on back to his cabin. He shut the cabin door behind him and quickly opened his suitcase, rummaging around in it until his hand felt the cool hard handle of his Smith and Wesson. He jerked the gun from holster, thrust it under the waistband of his trousers.

The unexpectedness of the *Belle*'s whistle signal had emptied the lounge tables and the long room was deserted as Ned crossed it and left it by its wide front doorway. As he came on the deck he saw Carry standing alongside her chair peering toward the near bank.

Excitement was crowding him as he strode up to her, reached out and laid a hand on her shoulder and turned her about. Her oval face took on a look of chill aloofness when she saw who it was. She was about to say something when he cut her short.

"Carry, this'll have to be quick and you've got to listen. That whistle was signaling Tom and Will. Hargutt sighted them off there about a mile away. Now —"

"Will?" she cried softly. "He's all right?"

Her look of radiant happiness was a galling thing for Ned to have to witness. Yet he did his best to ignore it in the face of something extremely urgent. "He is. Carry, they've got a man with them. It's Matt Kelso."

"Kelso?" She was incredulous. "How can that be?"

"Here's how. I've finally hit on the answer to all this . . . to who robbed the wagon last night and robbed both our stages. It has to be Lyle Danbo."

Carry's striking face was slack in astonishment. Ned gave her no chance to say anything, hurrying on, "Don't you see? Everything fits. Danbo was the man that recommended my hiring Kelso and Worts. Nothing had ever happened to our stages before those two came with the crew. By that time Danbo had made me his offer to buy into the outfit. I trusted him. He knew about every express box that carried gold. Do you see how it adds up? Now I could cut my tongue out for that slip I made about Will."

"You mean . . . Danbo let Kelso know when gold was going out? He —"

"That's it exactly." Ned half turned now to peer down along the deck, his glance closely examining the scattering of passengers lining the rail. Danbo wasn't among them, and he turned back to Carry to say quickly, "You and I are the only ones that know so far what all that whistling meant. I was up above with Hargutt when he sighted Will and Tom and Kelso. Now I want you to come with me."

He pulled his coat aside so that she could see the handle of the gun showing above his belt.

"We're going to take care of Lyle right now. Arrest him. You're to hear what he has to say. If we wait, if he lays eyes on Tom and Will and Kelso, he could make a run for it and get away."

The girl's eyes were wide open in alarm. "But, Ned, how can —"

"There's no time to lose," he cut in, reaching out to take her hand and pull her away from the rail. "Come along."

She let him guide her across and past the stairway to the far side. And as they turned down along the deck, Ned seeing only two people between him and the deck's end — neither of them Danbo — told her, "He wasn't inside. So he's either up above or down below. Let's try it above first."

They took the forward ladder to the hurricane, Ned leading the way. The instant his head rose above the level of that upper deck he saw Lyle Danbo standing alongside the wheelhouse, back turned. He finished the climb, turned to take Carry's arm and silently pointed toward the gambler.

Carry took a tight hold on his arm and he reached down to push her hand away, saying softly, "Stay close to me," as he started for the wheelhouse.

He and Carry were some thirty feet from the wheelhouse when either a warning instinct or something Hargutt told him made the gambler face around. His right hand held the brass telescope, and he reached out and handed the glass to Hargutt, a slow smile touching his face as he tipped his hat.

"You've heard the news I take it. Good news, isn't it? But isn't that Matt Kelso they've got with them?"

Danbo's unruffled manner only heightened Ned's seething anger. Ned this moment was looking upon a man who had coolly outwitted him, made a fool of him. And it was that deep chagrin blended with his mounting rage that made him cast aside all caution and say hotly, "Sure it's Kelso, Lyle. He's your man, isn't he? The one that helped you with the stage across in Leesville the other night. The one that wouldn't put up a fight when his stage was stopped last week with that box of Red Byrd's aboard."

Danbo was for once held speechless by hard surprise. And as he stood there staring incredulously at Ned, a voice calling from the river's near bank sounded across to them.

It was Tom Knight who had hailed the *Belle*. Danbo looked beyond Ned and saw Knight, followed by Kelso and Will, pushing through a tangle of willows scarcely two hundred yards away.

Hargutt was spinning the wheel and turning the *Belle*'s blunt bow in toward the bank then as Danbo drawled, "So you've found yourself a corner you can't crawl out of, eh, Ned?"

"I've put you in one you can't crawl out of, you mean!"

Ned's ego was bolstered by the sure conviction that the only weapon the gambler ever carried was a derringer and by a firm belief that Danbo couldn't possibly be expert in the use of the weapon.

The gambler's glance strayed briefly to Carry now. "Miss Knight, your friend here has a loose tongue. But not loose enough to tell you all he knows. Get him to tell you about last night, about —"

He was staring full at Ned now. He saw the man's muscles suddenly tighten, saw the fingers of Ned's right hand claw and stiffen. That telltale sign warned him of what was coming, let him anticipate the upward lift of Ned's right arm.

His own right hand slashed in under his coat with superb sureness and came out fisting the derringer. He had a full second in which to line the weapon upon the panicked Ned, a deliberate second in which to think what a fool Ned had been to approach him so closely that a miss with his short-range weapon was nigh to impossible. He even had the time to marvel at Ned not lunging behind the girl.

Then he squeezed the trigger.

The derringer's sharp blast pounded Ned backward, buckling at the waist. His eyes came wide open in disbelief and amazement. He stumbled hard into Carry, who cried out, "Oh, Ned!" the instant his knees gave way.

He fell heavily to the deck, the gun spinning from his hand. His eyes were beginning to glaze over as Danbo stooped quickly and picked up his gun.

The gambler spun around then, calling curtly to Hargutt, "Get this thing away from that bank!"

Will had a minute ago sighted Carry and Ned and Danbo on the *Belle*'s hurricane. The packet was nosing in toward the bank as he turned to Tom to say, "When we get there you keep an eye on our friend here while I go aboard."

"You're to wait for me, Will. We'll all three —"

The sound of a gunshot from out on the river cut across Tom's words. Will looked out to the packet in time to see Ned crumple loosely to the deck. The *Belle* was fifty feet short of the bank but still closing on it.

An instant alarm threaded Will's nerves even before he saw Carry kneel on the deck alongside Ned and Danbo walk quickly to the wheelhouse. Suddenly he made out the gun in Danbo's hand. Raking the barrel of his horse with the sharp-roweled spurs he had borrowed from Kelso, he ran on ahead of the other two.

He had halved the distance between him and the *Belle* when the packet's wheel slowed to a stop, then began churning the water in reverse. The boat was still edging toward the bank, barely twenty feet out from it, and he rammed home the spurs again to send the bay horse on at a harder run.

He leaned back against the reins as he came even with the stern-wheeler's blunt bow. It was inching outward from the bank now. He threw himself from the saddle, stumbled down the high bank and stepped into the mud. He felt his boots sinking into the mire and dove out into deeper water, feeling his right boot pull free of his foot.

A pair of roustabouts had seen him and were now running forward along the main deck. He struck out powerfully, closing on the packet's rounded bow at first. But then he seemed to be motionless in the water even though he was putting all his strength into the flailing of his arms. And finally, inch by inch, he saw the *Belle* drawing away from him and began feeling the weight of his clothes and Kelso's heavy shell belt and gun.

All at once a man's shape loomed above the line of the packet's squat hull and a coil of rope sailed straight out at him. He caught the rope, wound it about his wrist and felt himself pulled through the water. Then the roustabout was hauling strongly on the line to pull him closer.

In five more seconds he reached up, caught a hold on the thick coaming timber and hauled himself out of the water. He sprawled belly-down on the splintered planks and lay a moment gasping, dragging air into his lungs. A hand roughly pulled him farther on the deck, helped him to his feet, and he stared into the roustabout's unshaven face to say, "Thanks, friend."

"What's goin' on here?" the man wanted to know.

"Tell you later."

Will pushed on past, leaving a trail of water behind him as he ran for the main stairway, followed by the glances of upward of a dozen of the crew who had witnessed his being hauled out of the river.

Will, coming to the head of the stairs, lunged for the cabin corner on the riverward side of the deck and, a pace beyond, stepped onto the ladder leading to the hurricane. His first glimpse of that upper deck showed him Carry kneeling alongside Ned's sprawled body and, standing on the wheelhouse platform, Lyle Danbo.

The gambler was peering off toward the river bank, and Will had climbed from the ladder head and was reaching to holster before the gambler noticed him and, lightning-fast, lined the derringer at him.

Will halted, let his hand fall empty from holster. Even across this distance of perhaps fifty feet he could see indecision creep into Danbo's glance. And he suddenly knew the man was realizing that the range was far too great for him to be sure of his short-barreled weapon throwing its bullet true.

"Want to give it a try?" Will called. And now, deliberately, he let his right hand lift to the handle of the .44 once more.

The next instant he saw his mistake. For Danbo, smiling suddenly, arced his weapon around and into line with Carry. The sound of Will's voice had made the girl turn. She was staring at him with a look of wide-eyed thankfulness thinning her alarm.

Yet now as Will's dark face tightened in apprehension at the gambler's move, Carry turned her head to see the derringer lined at her. Her face lost color then as Danbo called, "Don't make me use this, Speer!"

Those words took Will back to that morning when he had felt the same weapon's twin barrels touching the back of his neck in the stage office. Danbo had been a dangerous man then; he was even more dangerous now.

"Hargutt, move her ahead now! And fast!"

The gambler's words were crisp, toneless and deadly. A moment later Will heard the ring of the engine room bell below and felt the pulsating throb of the big paddle wheel at the stern abruptly stop. Then, with Danbo still staring hard at Carry over the barrel of the derringer, the paddle wheel's beat commenced once more, moving the *Belle* slowly ahead against the pull of the river's sluggish current.

Lyle Danbo coolly waited out a quarter-minute interval until the packet had gained headway. Then he all at once stepped down off the wheelhouse platform, saying crisply, "Hargutt, get out here!"

His glance briefly shuttled to Will as Hargutt appeared out of the wheelhouse. "Don't make a try for your gun, Speer," he said. And then slowly, watching Will, he began pacing backward past the Texas along the deck. Ten paces took him to the hurricane's far back corner. He stopped there. And abruptly his gun arm slowly dropped to his side and he was saying, "You two make a fine pair. Miss Knight, I've done you a favor. Shooting down that cur was a thing someone should have done long ago."

That moment Will saw Fred Hargutt's weathered face tighten in alarm. The *Belle,* with no one at the wheel, was yawing around broadside to the current.

Will had perhaps a two-second awareness of what was happening before Danbo wheeled unexpectedly and leaped over the deck's edge.

The instant his falling shape disappeared, Will ran back along the deck. Carry was coming to her feet as he passed her. He was aware of Hargutt lunging for the wheelhouse door.

Hauling up short at the deck's edge, he gripped the handle of the .44. But then he hesitated, knowing that it wasn't in him to shoot a defenseless man, even Danbo, swimming for his life.

He stared below now seeing the roiled, foaming spot where the gambler's body had hit the water. It was even with the rounded stern of the hull, even with the boxed-in spray shield of the big paddle wheel. Danbo was nowhere in sight.

Suddenly the man's head bobbed to the surface a few feet out from the churning heavy planks of the wheel. Carry came alongside Will that moment, taking a tight hold on his arm. He wanted to look around at her. But his stare was held fascinated as he realized that the whirling blades of the big wheel were swinging around on Danbo.

He bellowed in hard alarm, "Watch out! Swim!"

Perhaps Danbo heard him, for now he struck out with both arms, frantically trying to pull himself clear of those whirling broad planks.

But the suction of that roiled water drew him backward and down. And Will quickly reached out to put an arm about Carry and hold her head against his chest.

He stood there bleakly watching, hoping for a glimpse of Danbo out beyond reach of the paddle wheel, turning Carry away from the sight as she stood with her face against his wet shirt front. He could feel her trembling.

After a minute had passed, after Hargutt had managed to work the packet's bow around against the current, Will knew that they had seen the last of the gambler. For nothing but a creamy froth of muddy river water showed along the *Belle*'s ragged wake.

The night was chill, the stars made a brilliant delicate pattern against the ebony void of the heavens.

Will and Carry stood between the *Belle*'s high twin stacks along the dark expanse of the hurricane. The muted sound of voices drifted up from the saloon below and the broad expanse of the river was patterned in rippling bars of reflected lantern light.

Neither of them had spoken a word over the past five minutes. Yet now Carry turned abruptly to Will and looked up at him to say softly, "Will, I did love Ned. You must know that. But it was the Ned you and I knew long ago, before . . ."

Will waited for her to finish. When she didn't he gently told her, "That's the Ned I want to remember. They never come any finer. Never."

Something in his words made her put her arm through his and press it tightly to her breast. Then a moment later she swung around to face him, to reach up and run her hands along his cheek in a feathery caress as his arms came about her.